MW01088514

on

Maruba Island

Bahama Romance Series

Teri M. Bethel

Copyrights

Acknowledgments

I could not have done this without the tireless support of my amazing, loving husband, Tellis. I love you, forever…

Dedication

To my precious nieces Lauren Wong, Ariana Vanderpool-Wallace, Chelsea Wong, Laura Knowles, Britni Knowles, Erica Knowles, Alexa Delaney, Ariana Delaney, and Hannah Bethel... that you may find pure and lasting love.

Contents

~Chapter One~

J ennifer Hanna raced down the dirt path toward old Aunt Bessie's house. It was high noon, and the fierce island sun beat relentlessly on her uncovered head. Despite her vigorous motion, not a strand of hair moved—partially because of the dirt that was compressed in her hair and clothes as she tussled at the water pump moments before.

Today there was not even a hint of a fresh breeze to cool her sun-scorched neck. Apart from the occasional shade from the red and green Poinciana trees that lined the uneven island road, there was no relief as sweat poured down her chocolate brown skin.

Passersby tooted the horns of their old cars for her to move on the side as they made their way through the narrow street. The drivers were not the least bit moved by a fourteen-year-old girl toting two good size pails of water. The village pump in the middle of town would soon be alight with children making multiple trips to collect water to cart home to their families.

There were virtually no new cars on Maruba, a little island in the Bahama chain of islands. All were left-hand drives and drove on the left side of the road. Not that it really mattered much with the narrow streets, but the law was that drivers were to keep left.

The cars weren't anything fancy. For the most part, they were old beat up looking 1938 Dodge cars brought in from the mainland on a shipping barge that stopped by at least three times a year to deliver cars or large equipment and merchandise. Most of them looked the same except they were either silver or a light blue color with a green double-digit license plate with white numbers that read Maruba on top and Bahamas at the bottom.

The natives walked, rode their bicycles, or a tired old mule to work their farms. To have a car was a matter of luxury, even if it was really old.

"I've got to make it back before Daddy gets home," Jenny murmured as she tried unsuccessfully to contain the water that swirled from the two buckets in her hand.

The last time Jenny came too late, she tasted her father's wrath. If she had any hopes of eating lunch today, she would have to do so before he found some reason to lash out at her. Jenny recalled yesterday's fiasco. By now, the whole village remembered it. As usual, her life was the talk of the town.

Despite the idyllic surrounding on the quaint tropical island in the West Indies, Jenny's life was like the water in her bucket—a virtual swirling frenzy. Jenny wondered how she would avoid her aunt, who stood waiting for her today. Aunt Bessie was always angry, which didn't do anything to help her already frightening features. Her face had a permanent scowl that just drew attention to the age lines around her pursed dark brown lips and her piercing black eyes. Her body looked as though she had a lumpy woolen blanket permanently wrapped around her mid-section under a well-aged cotton shift. The fact that most of her teeth were slightly twisted yet had enough space to accommodate at least two grains of cooked rice did not help to soften Bessie's features at all.

Jenny's mind drifted to the events of the day before. She had been late again with the buckets of water. It didn't matter that she had to make several trips to the pump to fill their galvanized tubs. She was expected to have them filled before her daddy Nat Hanna left for work every morning. Nat fumed as he barged onto the front porch and emptied her meager portion of food onto the rocky ground below.

"If you know what's good for you, Girl, you'd make haste with y'chores," Nat bawled at her.

Of course, that was before she had a chance to explain why she was late. It didn't matter much; in any event, Jenny was terrified of her daddy. Though his beady left eye was fixed on her, his right eye always looked as if it were checking out someone way up in a coconut tree. If that weren't bad enough, his voice thundered, causing the hair on her neck to stand up.

"I done told you, Girl, if you don't earn your keep, you'll eat with the dog," he shouted for the entire settlement to hear before storming back inside the clapboard house.

As humiliated as Jenny was at the time, her empty stomach gnawed at her, overriding all sense of shame. Before their scruffy dog decided to devour her lunch, Jenny bolted down the steps and converged on the food. Seconds later, she was seeking refuge in her favorite spot under the propped-up three-bedroom house with Rover. Jenny glanced at the dog, who seemed to have a pitiful look on his face. He was the closest thing she had to a friend.

"It ain't so bad, Rover, at least this time Daddy didn't whup me in front of the neighbors."

A short time later, Aunt Bessie stood at the front door with her arms folded across her broad stomach. She told her brother to stop throwing the child's food on the ground in front of the house.

"Supposin' the neighbors go and report us, Nat?" she fussed at him. Bessie knew how news traveled quickly on the island, and before you knew it, some nitwit from the Social Service Department would be banging on their door asking questions.

"Ain't nobody's biz'ness what I do in my house, Woman!" Nat scowled.

Nat was so comfortable in Bessie's house that he had taken to calling it his own for years. Bessie made a mental note to refresh his memory when his passion had cooled down some. When it came to

Nat and his daughter, Bessie knew that she was treading on fiery ground.

That was yesterday. Today Jenny had been gone only an hour, though it felt like two, as she stood in line at the timeworn neighborhood pump across from the local marketplace. The other kids laughed at her as she shifted from foot to foot, anxiously waiting for her turn at the pump. Jenny looked as though she was the last in a line of twenty at the outdoor toilet with very little chance of relieving herself before the inevitable happened. Her expression was one of desperation.

Almost everybody in town had to collect their water from the local pump. There was no running water or electricity in any of the houses in the village except for some of the richer folks who lived on the hill or on the outskirts of town like the Fords, the Albury's, and a few other white families. A good amount of the locals who lived further inland were fortunate to have their own water pumps as well as rainwater collection bins.

All the village kids had chores just like she did, but their folks didn't have a hankerin' to whup them every day. Most of the older folks were already tending to their crops before daybreak and expected the household chores to be done by the time they returned home. That left quite a bit of time to get things done, especially in homes with four and five kids to share the chores. But there was only Jenny in her home with her dad and old aunt. So much of the house chores and some of the field chores rested squarely on her little shoulders.

Some of the kids played on the swing across the street. They took turns pushing each other back and forth on the used truck tire attached by a rope to an overhanging branch of the large shade tree.

Everyone in the village knew about Jenny's mean family, but it didn't stop them from teasing her. Blake Smith was the main contender; his father knew Jenny's daddy well. In fact, it was Mr. Smith who made it his business to inform the entire settlement of the affairs in Jenny's home. Not that he had to, Nat never tried to hide his distaste for his daughter.

4

"Oh, you're gonna get another whuppin,' Girl," Blake squawked as he turned the tap low to a virtual drizzle as Jenny waited in line.

"Not half as bad as you're gonna get from me if you don't hurry up, Blake Smith!" Jenny railed at him shaking her fist in the air.

The other kids laughed. This seemed the high point of their day. Blake always provoked Jenny at the pump, and though she was a spindly looking girl, Jenny was full of fire. Her big almond-shaped eyes would light up when she was about to get in a tussle with Blake. It wasn't long before some passerby had to literally peel Jenny from Blake's back.

Today was no different. Jenny rode Blake like an untamed stallion, grabbing, biting, and pounding him until, as always, someone intervened. Now her overalls were muddy, and her coarse stubby plaits rerouted themselves to stick out like grizzly mud-covered spears of an African warrior. But that was small things compared to what Blake looked like.

~Chapter Two~

"**H**urry up, Child," her pudgy aunt bellowed at her. "I gat somethin' for ya!" Aunt Bessie stood on the porch anxiously waiting for Jenny's return.

Jenny knew all too well what that was, but today she had just about as much licks as she could take. Her aunt stood briskly, hitting the thin switch from the old tamarind tree in her hand, stopping only to shift a tight curler that peeped from her multi-colored floral headscarf.

"Didn't I tell you to be back with the water before my spit dried?" she hollered at her niece, causing their neighbors to take note of their private affairs one more time.

Jenny grunted a reply under her breath, acknowledging her aunt's question. Why the old bat just didn't buy a watch like most people was beyond her understanding. Besides, there wasn't much spit on the rock today. If the old buzzard had a cold, her spit wouldn't dry up so fast!

"Hmph," Jenny huffed, "Aunt Bessie just had a hankerin' to whup someone." She dropped the buckets at her aunt's feet, splashing a little of its contents on her broad uncovered toes. "Not today, you old buzzard," Jenny whispered as she jumped off the porch and scurried under the old propped-up clapboard house. "I'd rather spend the day with my friend."

Jenny crawled on her belly to Rover, who was fixed on spending most of his day escaping the heat as usual, underneath Aunt Bessie's house. For most of the neighbors, the show was over until the next time. Unfortunately, pulling up a big rock next to their old rickety tin roof houses to watch Jenny was the next best thing to a picture show for the less-occupied stragglers.

Just as Jenny was about to come out from hiding, Aunt Bessie bolted out of the house with thunderous speed. She was all dressed up in her funeral black with a sad look pasted across her freshly powdered face. Her head was free of the pink sponge hair curlers, which seemed to be a permanent fixture to her head nowadays, even if she had nowhere to go.

"Where y' goin', Aunt Bessie?" Jenny asked, dusting herself off as she scrambled from the rubble where she had hidden under the house with the dog.

"Now that's a foolish question. Can't you hear the drums? There's a funeral in town, an' I have ta pay my respects." Jenny grinned—her aunt never missed a funeral—don't care who was in the box.

"Well, you sure look grieved. Have a nice time," Jenny coaxed the older lady.

"Oh, thanks, child, but I do hope it ain't nobody I know thas' passed."

Ever since Jenny knew her auntie, it was talked through the town that Bessie-Mae Francis was the settlement's faithful funeral finder. She could never pass up a good cry. Course, she had to see who was in the box and what they had on so that she could be in the know when the locals gathered in the backyard to gossip about the day's events. Aunt Bessie always complained that the place just wasn't the same as in years gone by when you knew everyone on the island.

It was times like this that Jenny believed that there was a God. Cause it was surely His miraculous hands that got her aunt to forget the licks she was about to pan out on her l'il backside earlier. God wasn't such a big deal in her family since April 7, 1958. That was the day Jenny was born. Since that day, Nat Hanna believed God had gone on vacation. She heard it many times before. By now, it was no secret.

"If it wasn't for that l'il nappy head, broad lip girl, my wife would still be here with us today," her daddy scowled.

Nat Hanna had always been a quarrelsome boisterous man. He wasn't much to look at. But if you could just excuse his face, his body was good an' strong. Just what the women thought was needful of a family man.

A fisherman by profession, Nat had doted on Jenny's mother. He claimed she was the best thing that ever happened to him since the gov'ment built the dock in the harbor next to the marketplace. In fact, when he married Muffin Pratt, Nat put aside all his vices. He stopped drinking, gambling, and even fighting in the street. He claimed he gave it all up for his beauty.

Well, all except womanizin', that was one thing even Muffin stayed on her knees about. But she did get him to go to church to listen to Rev. Mackey. Surprisingly, Rev. was talking sense, according to Nat. If only he would get the right-sized teeth to fit his mouth, more people would sit in the front of the church without fear of experiencing intermittent showers.

~Chapter Three~

"OOOh, oooh, oooh," **Muffin** gasped as she felt her contractions heighten. It was two o'clock in the day, and the baby pressed hard against Muffin's womb. She knew it was time. "Lawdy, this one is hot!" she glanced around the little room to find something to brace her up as she gripped her stomach.

Muffin considered herself a pro by now. She even figured she could deliver her baby all by herself. This was, after all, her thirteenth child and, oh, how she doted on her children. This one was a little more active than the others, however. Muffin couldn't remember any of her children slowing her down like this one. Even Jasper, her only boy child, wasn't so uncomfortable despite his hefty size.

Bessie was the first to figure it out. Muffin was pregnant. She had gained a whole lot of weight and had slowed down a bit, but you couldn't see the typically projected stomach. Her sister-in-law was about seven months along when it was confirmed that she was pregnant. Now she was walking around huffing and tooting like a choo choo train.

"Could be 'cause you done put on sixty-five pounds with this one." Bessie was always quick to remind Muffin of the weight she had acquired through the years.

When Muffin and Nat were married, she weighed less than 150 pounds. Now twenty-three years later, it looked as though she had doubled her weight. Nat didn't care; he loved his Muffin no matter what size she was. Muffin was the kind of girl who could melt ice cream with a smile, but if you crossed her path, she would not hesitate to scold you.

"What you think I should do, Bessie?" she fired back at her sister-in-law, "starve my babies! It jus' ain't right growin' no sickly lookin' chilren."

Bessie thought not to push the point any further. She knew her brother's wife well enough to know how far to go with Muffin. Since they came to live with her in her little house, she often had a taste of Muffin's tongue lashin' and came even closer to getting a good walloping.

Muffin stooped low on the weathered plank floor.

"Ooh," she cried out. "This l'il one tryin' to get out, Bessie, it's time!"

Bessie grabbed her sister-in-law by the arm and guided her to her bed across the creaky wood plank floor.

"Time or no time, my friend, you ain't messin' up my clean floor. Now you jus' set yourself here until I call for help."

Within the hour, Ms. Clarabel, the midwife, was beside Muffin, coaching her and preparing for the baby's arrival. Clarabel was a faithful soul in her community. She had delivered most of the kids in the settlement for the last ten years or so. Before that, she worked in the hospital on the Mainland and only moved to the island after her husband passed. Since she could never have any children of her own, Clarabel helped the women on the island have healthy babies.

"Relax, Muffin," she encouraged her, "breathe deep but slow." Ms. Clarabel could see that Muffin was already getting tired. She promised to lose some of her excess weight before having another baby, but that never happened.

"You relax; I'll take care of the rest." Ms. Clarabel wiped the sweat from Muffin's forehead. Muffin knew she could depend on Ms. Clarabel; she was delivering babies for years and had brought seven of Muffin's children into the world. This one would be no different.

Three hours passed, and still, the infant had not made its way out. Bessie lit the lamp in the room and pulled the window shut. It was hot, but she was afraid the smoke from the neighbors burning garbage would make Muffin uncomfortable. The night was still. The usual sweet-smelling air from the ocean was blocked by the neighbor's burning trash in his 55-gallon tin drum.

"This one taking its time coming out, Muffin." Bessie sighed as she peeped through the room door, trying to keep track of Muffin and Nat at the same time as he paced back and forth on the front porch.

The midwife turned to Bessie, waving for her to shut the door. Bessie had been in and out of the room to check on her sister-in-law, but she was more of a distraction than a help. Nat came as soon as he got word that the baby was coming. Now he wasn't so interested in the baby. It was his wife he was concerned for. Minutes later, a loud shrill rang through the little clapboard house, sending shivers down Nat's spine as Muffin gave her best effort to push her baby out.

Bessie gurgled a throaty laugh. Muffin ate everything in sight for the last nine months and was as big as a beached whale. Only thing was, the baby was a long scrawny girl with barely any weight on her at all, except for her lips that sprawled across her narrow face.

"So much for eatin' for two," she said, grinning at the thin child. Bessie turned to Muffin, who lay listlessly on the bed.

"You gat yourself another girl Muffin," Bessie informed her sister-in-law as she looked over Ms. Clarabel's shoulder. "This is the little terror that gave you all that trouble."

Muffin gave a tired smile as Ms. Clarabel placed the child in her arms.

"This child ain't no terror, Bessie," she whispered, "her name is Jennifer Albertha Hanna, and she's a gift from God."

Little Jenny cried as her mother grappled to catch her breath on the sweat-drenched bed. Nat came into the dimly lit room, not even bothering to look at his child, who had already been passed to her aunt. After Clarabel had cleaned up the infant, she gave Bessie some instructions for the infant then quietly slipped out of the room to deliver another baby. Her days were busier since the doctor cut his visits to the island down to three days every two weeks. The nurse in the clinic had her hands full with the daily running of the place, so all the birthing was left to Clarabel. This was her fifth delivery in four days.

"Hey, Muffin, you alright?" Nat asked as he wiped her forehead.

Muffin gave Nat a tired smile. He could see she was exhausted, but he had never seen her quite so listless before.

"We did good eh Nat, we gat ourselves another baby," she whispered.

Nat hovered over his wife almost an hour without even checking on his baby. He had never seen Muffin like this before. He always told her that she was a good breeder, but now she lay fading before his eyes. Bessie tried to give Nat little Jenny, but he refused to hold her. He was too concerned for his wife.

After thirteen children, Nat knew his wife well enough to recognize that something was wrong. He didn't know what it was and had no way of fixing the problem. Nat knelt down next to his wife and kissed her cheek. Muffin turned her head towards him slightly and tried to whisper to him. He couldn't hear her, but he knew pretty well what she was saying. She had done it so many times when she brought his lunch to him at the dock. While his customers were haggling with him for better prices on the fish, she would bend over in all her fullness, wink at him, and soundlessly mouth her famous "I love you, Baby." If that didn't cause him to melt, the rolling walk down the wharf did. Before he knew it, he was yielding to his customer's offer, just wanting to sell all of his fish to get home to his wife.

Nat felt when his wife's hand went limp after she gasped for her last breath. He was just about to pray but didn't know how to. His breath seemed to almost backtrack on him, causing him to choke. Nat gripped his wife's hand and shook her gently.

"No, no, Muff, ya can't go now. Remember the things we plan to do?" he shook her head gently, trying to wake her, but her breath had gone even though her eyes remained open.

"Muff—Muff, don't you leave me now. I'll take care of you, Muff. You see, me and Bessie will take care of you. You don't have to worry bout a thing."

Nat thought of all the things he wanted to say to his wife. He wanted to tell her thanks for all the good she had been to him and their family. He wanted her to hear him say, "I love you, Muffin." She had told it to him almost every day of their lives together, but he was tough. He was a man, and men didn't say that. That would be a sign of weakness. Muffin was the best thing that ever happened to him. Without thinking about who was with him, he flung himself over his dead wife, howling like a wounded animal releasing much of the anguish he felt deep inside. Even Bessie cried, but not for Muffin. Her tears were for her brother. She had never seen him or any other man so broken before. It felt like her heart was too heavy to breathe. She could only imagine what her brother felt. Muffin was his life.

The kerosene lamp began to flicker in the little room. Most of the oil had been used up, and the flame was about to go out. Bessie took Jenny into her room. She placed a pillow on the floor mat and positioned the infant on it while she went in search of a can of cream and water for her first meal.

It was then that Nat started drinking again. Every time he looked at his daughter, he remembered losing Muffin. His memories of his wife became even more inflated the more he drank. As the years passed, his memories were less accurate, but his hatred for

Jenny grew. Nat did his best not to acknowledge the child's presence. It was left to Bessie to raise Jenny now. She figured someone had to look after the child even though she and Muffin didn't get along with each other so well.

None of Nat's older children cared to have the child. Most of them claimed they had enough trouble with their own. They figured if their old pa could find time to make bones, he should find a way to take care of it!

Even though Muffin loved her children, the family was not a close-knit, caring one. Each had gone their separate ways. Muffin spilled out babies like a machine, and she loved each one, though they didn't all get the attention and guidance of loving parents. Nat saw himself as the provider, and the rest was left to Muffin. Whatever the rest was, he didn't have a clue. As far as he was concerned, they had enough food for a belly full with the farm and his fishing. When the kids grew up, they quickly moved out of their cramped surroundings and went in search of a better life on the mainland.

The youngest of Jenny's siblings was Brazella, who, at age sixteen, ran off with sweet-talkin' Silas Bain to live on the mainland. Brazella knew that if she had stayed on the island, her daddy would've half-killed her when he found out that she was pregnant for her rovin' renegade. With the mainland some 60 miles or so from Maruba, Brazella figured she was safe from her daddy's reach since he never left his island home.

A couple of months into the marriage Brazella lost her baby while fighting with Silas over his new sweetheart. All of Muffin's older children had been long gone, leaving Jenny to fend for herself. Life with Nat and Bessie was nothing short of torturous.

14

~Chapter Four~

Fourteen years later, and Nat had not softened a bit. He had adjusted to not having Muffin around, but he still did not come to terms with Jenny. The resentment he had for his daughter spiraled to an uncontrollable level. It got so that Nat didn't even remember why he hated the girl; he figured he just didn't need a reason.

It wasn't that she was a bad girl. In fact, if he were honest with himself, he would see that she was quite a young lady. The talk around the village was that the child had a hankerin' for learnin' too. Something quite foreign to both Nat and Bessie. In Nat's mind, children were bred to work. They were an investment—nothing more. According to Blake Smith's father, the day Nat Hanna gave Jenny the time of day—would be the day chicken grew teeth!

Mr. Smith had been Nat's drinking buddy for many years. He believed that he knew the man inside out. As far as Jenny was concerned, that was no big feat. There just wasn't much happening with her father, don't care if it was inside or out. Nothin' plus nothin' still equaled nothin' in Jenny's books; her daddy just didn't make the mark by any stretch of the imagination. But that didn't stop Jenny from being respectful and carrying her weight around the house.

In Nat's home growing up, affection was not something you displayed. His daddy didn't do it, and neither did his granddaddy. It

15

was a man's thing on the islands. Women, well, they were for breeding, tending the children, and entertainment. According to grampy anyway, if you let them get too close, it could just get your emotions all kerpuncalated.

It wasn't that Nat was such a catch that he could pick and choose which women he wanted to have. But he did have something going for himself. It wasn't his good looks, cause he sure didn't have any... and it wasn't his money cause he was too cheap to buy his own house. Nat chose to live with his sister and squeeze up to six children at a time in one bedroom with an old rank, pee-stained, king-size mattress on the floor. No, the girls were after Nat because, in their minds, they saw the potential to have money. He was a fit young man who, at a young age, had his very own fishing boat. Now, on Maruba, that was a catch.

Nat always remembered what his old grampy had told him about women. "Son, y'jus gatta tame 'em; an' only one way to do dat." Nat would smile cause he had heard his grampy say it a million times. "Keep 'em pregnant, barefoot, innorant, and livin' in fear."

That didn't work so much on Muffin, except the pregnant part. Muffin was a giant of a lady. She was almost as wide as she was tall and had a humongous size heart to match. She was a woman dedicated to her family. Where Nat lacked in affection, Muffin dished it out in double doses.

She didn't take too much to people commenting on her size though. Muffin called herself a big-boned lady, which accounted for the size of her body. But that didn't bother Nat any, he didn't want no woman that could easily break. He needed a workhorse, a big one. One that could breed good chilren, tend to his family and help run the farm. Now it didn't hurt that Muffin could roll them big bones when she walked too. Oh, no, in Nat's eyes, Muffin was a good lookin' woman.

Jenny didn't know anything about her mother. There was no talk of her around her, and laughter ceased in the house when Muffin died. Since Muffin was gone and Jenny was here, she would have to take up some of the slack around the house. Work started for Jenny from she was four years going on five. Though she didn't have to lift the buckets back then, Jenny made regular trips to the pump, collecting water for her family in gallon size containers.

But that didn't stop Nat from instilling a hearty dose of fear in his daughter. "If she knew what was good for her," Nat seethed almost daily, "she would tend to her chores."

Jenny knew quite well what her father meant. He made it a practice to threaten her jus' to keep her on her toes. When he was good and ready, he would strap her with his belt. Nat figured if he instilled enough fear in her, she would do exactly what he wanted, how and when he wanted it. Bessie was in complete agreement. She figured in her old age, it was time for some payback on lookin' after her brother's child. But if Jenny wanted to waste her time goin' to school an' fillin' her nappy head with flowedy thoughts, that was her biz'ness. She didn't mind so long as Jenny finished her work.

That's exactly what Jenny did. She worked hard and long, never once complaining to her aunt about the tasks she had ladened her with. After her morning chores, Jenny would race with her only pair of shoes in hand to the one-room school building, hoping to get some schooling before her daddy returned from fishing or drinking—whatever was his fancy that day.

Jenny was a naturally bright child who was fortunate to have an understanding teacher. Teachers on the island often taught all levels. The schools were something like a one-size-fits-all kind of school. The school in Jenny's village was called Maruba All-Age School. They had one teacher for the whole school. Because Maruba was a British Colony, it was from Great Britain most of the teachers came from. That's where Jenny's teacher, Ms. Trotman, was from.

She had come in from England a few years before and was one of the few white folks who lived on their island on the outskirts of their little village; she lived in a government cottage with a generator for electricity and indoor water. Ms. Trotman knew nothing much of the islanders or their way of life, but she managed to win the respect of most of the parents and the love of the children.

The school was set close to the waterfront and surrounded by green fields. Mostly bananas were grown on the island, but everyone dabbled in other fruit and vegetables to keep food in their pots. There was hardly a property that didn't grow pigeon peas, corn, bananas, and sweet potatoes. In the evenings, most of the older folks would gather on the porch to shell their peas to send to the mainland on the mailboat. The youngsters played in the dirt yard in front of the house.

There was no such thing as a packed lunch for Jenny or many of the kids. It was a matter of picking the fresh guavas and plums from the trees that had sprung up on the side of the road as they walked to school. If, by chance, there was some freshly fried bread leftover from breakfast, it was packed for a later snack for school if Aunt Bessie wanted to share it. When she could, Jenny left home early enough to pick some fruit from the side of the road for her lunch. Meat was scarce in Jenny's home. When they did have it she had the leftover fat from her daddy's porkchop if Aunt Bessie was feeling generous. Otherwise except for the fish, Jenny's diet was vegetarian before islanders knew what a vegetarian diet was.

In the clearing across from the school was Jenny's favorite hangout place. Hardly any of the other kids went there; it was quiet and peaceful. Jenny loved to layout under the giant Poinciana trees and watch as the orange and red flowers drifted to the ground with the slightest breeze. The older kids would come there at times to read their books just as Ms. Trotman had suggested, so Jenny thought it an excellent idea for her to do as well.

Oftentimes, Jenny cut her classwork short to finish her farming chores before nightfall. Since she had a standing agreement with Aunt Bessie, she was permitted to go to school with the other children if she kept up with her chores. If, on the other hand, Jenny did not live up to these expectations, she would have to give up the schooling, plus tote a good whuppin'! It was as simple as that.

Jenny understood why she had to help with the farming though. When the boat came from the mainland, if Aunt Bessie didn't have any fresh or dried pigeon peas to send to Mr. Albury at the cannery at least once a month, she would have missed an opportunity to make a few dollars. The other crops were sold too, but that went mainly to the government packing houses, and the farmers didn't get much money for that.

Though Ms. Trotman did not get involved too closely with the students, she did notice that Jenny had a keen interest in reading and learning. Ms. Trotman knew that the child had a rough home life, but she knew that it was not customary for the teacher to get involved in the student's personal life. So she did what she could to help Jenny from the schoolroom.

Whatever books she could get her hands on, she would pass them on to Jenny. Ms. Trotman had friends on the mainland send her books just so that Jenny could have a moment of enjoyment. It was her way of escaping the dark home she lived in.

"You're quite special, Jenny. A quick learner," Ms. Trotman told her. "You keep up the good work, and you will go far."

It was at school that Jenny felt alive. While other students spent their lunch breaks playing bat and ball, Jenny spent her break under the sprawling Poinciana tree in the schoolyard with any book she could get her hands on. Her favorites, though, were the full-color picture books. Reading was Jenny's way of escaping the little island of Maruba and traveling the world.

Although there were about fifty school-aged children in the settlement, many parents opted to keep their older children home to work the fields. Most of the kids thought it a great idea...but not Jenny. She believed that one day she would travel and be somebody important. The books she read gave her a glimpse of a world that she could one day be a part of. Jenny couldn't imagine wasting her time farming and toting water for the rest of her life.

~Chapter Five~

"**Eighteen years old and free** as a butterfly!" Jenny ran happily toward the marketplace. She had saved the few dollars made while taking care of old Ms. Chloé until she died last month. Ms. Chloé was a contentious old white woman from Maruba, but she was well off.

She even had running water in her big house on the hill. Most folks would've jumped at the money her grandson Thomas offered to look after his ailing grandmother. But after thinking long and hard, it was the general consensus that it was much better to be poor and broke than to work for the old coot. Of course, it was not a problem for Jenny. She told Thomas she was used to abuse.

"In fact," she said, trying to be funny, "if I didn't get beat once-in-awhile, I wouldn't know if I were livin'!"

Whatever her reason, Thomas Ford was grateful Jenny accepted the job. Ms. Chloé was miserable at first, living up to all the talk of her being the shriv'ly white witch of Ford Hill. But when she noticed that it didn't bother Jenny none, she just gave up and started being nice to the girl. Jenny was happy to be working for the Fords, she sang as she worked, and sometimes she even stayed a little longer, reading some of Thomas' books. Oftentimes, Thomas would bring home wonderful books that he thought Jenny might be interested in.

He looked forward to seeing her countenance brighten as they sat on the verandah, discussing their mutual findings in the books.

"Girl, come here," Ms. Chloé called her one day. "What's all that giggling for? Ain't you got some work to do?"

Jenny peeped her head around the door where Ms. Chloé lay in bed, all wrapped up in her blankets and her down comforter despite the heat that poured into the room.

Ms. Chloé's room was not like the typical island homes owned by the wealthy people in Maruba. Instead of the light, airy colors with a familiar splash of butternut yellow, Ms. Chloé's room was dark. The walls were painted a deep red color, and the furniture the darkest brown wood Jenny had ever seen. There was no tile anywhere in the house except in the bathrooms. All the floors were highly polished dark hardwood planks. Jenny loved Ms. Chloé's bed; she had so many pillows on the bed; it looked like she was being swallowed up. Her drapes and upholstery fabrics were a heavyweight damask fabric imported from Europe. The floral design on the fabric was predominantly a deep tan with splashes of red and green.

Walking into Ms. Chloé's room made you feel like someone was drawing you close and giving you a hug. Well, until Ms. Chloé spoke anyway. Then you felt like you were getting a throttling depending on what kind of mood she was in.

"Now, Ms. Chloé," Jenny answered her smiling, "you know that I already finish doing my work. I'm just reading now. Do you want me to read to you?"

Ms. Chloé managed to let a slight smile slip out.

"T'would be nice, Child. After all," she added quickly, "that is my book, and you are on my time."

As long as anything was in the house, even if Jenny brought it herself, Ms. Chloé claimed it as hers. Jenny learned not to nitpick with the ailing woman, at any rate. So long as Jenny didn't have to stop her reading, and so long as she didn't have to rush home to

Aunt Bessie's long sour face, Ms. Chloé's attempts to aggravate were just all right.

That was the start of Jenny and Ms. Chloé's famous relationship. Jenny made it a practice of reading to Ms. Chloé every afternoon, which meant having to stay a little later. When she would complete her chores, she would pull Ms. Chloé's posh French chair to her bedside to read to her.

If evening sneaked up on her, Jenny knew Thomas would give her a ride home. So if Jenny wasn't reading to Ms. Chloé, she was having chats with Thomas on the verandah of his hilltop home.

Before long, Thomas began finding reasons to come home earlier than usual. Though still relatively young, the weight of his responsibilities seemed to have aged him. Recently, despite his challenges, Thomas seemed to have uncapped a new vein of life, and he was beginning to feel alive once more. He began sharing his dreams with Jenny as though the two of them had a common mission. Jenny was intrigued with Thomas' plans, even though she didn't always fully grasp them. He had already started his 'little project,' as he called it, on the island's southwestern side. His family owned considerable acreage there, and Thomas planned to extend their hotel and marina and create a quaint shopping village for their elite clientele.

Jenny hoped that one day, she would visit Thomas' resort before she left the island. Truthfully, just like most of the people in the village, Jenny had barely moved from her tiny settlement in all of her seventeen years of life. Though Thomas was only eight years older than Jenny, she looked up to him and was amazed at his seemingly boundless intellect.

On his summer breaks from boarding school in Switzerland, Thomas was made to put all his schooling to good use in the family business. Shortly after graduating from University, he returned home to the island, having heard his parents were involved in a tragic accident in the company's seaplane, which took their lives. Since then, Thomas took over the business affairs and adopted his ailing grandmother, who lived by herself in the south.

Thomas had a few acquaintances that would pop in from time to time, but there was no noticeable lady in his life. At least none that came by the house while Jenny was there. For a dashingly handsome young man with such wealth, the people in the village all thought him a great catch for any young white woman. White men on the island just didn't marry black women even if they loved them more than the white.

But Jenny was different from most of the young ladies Thomas had known. She had a way of getting in and pulling your heart effortlessly towards her. Jenny wasn't the most beautiful person in the world to look at, although she had somewhat of an intriguingly exotic look. In any event, there was something about his housekeeper that made him drop his defenses and want to share his thoughts, ideas, and dreams with her. Both he and Ms. Chloé looked forward to Jenny's presence in their home.

While Jenny wasn't aware of it and neither was Thomas' grandmother, there was a marked difference in Ms. Chloé' since Jenny began working for them. Thomas noticed the drastic change in his grandmother within a few weeks. Ms. Chloé, who had been a trite sour with Thomas ever since his parent's death, was beginning to treat him kindly once again. Ms. Chloé looked forward to seeing her nurse-maid each day, sulking anytime Jenny had time off from work.

It did occur to Thomas on occasion that perhaps Jenny should move into the big house with them. However, he drove away the thought almost as quickly as it came. Thomas realized that he was becoming more emotionally involved with her daily, though Jenny was completely oblivious to his attraction. It was fine enough having Jenny in the house during the day. His grandmother would just have to adjust to not having her around in the evening. The villagers were already whispering about her long hours on the hill.

On the other hand, Jenny had no other notion in her head than working and saving her money to move away from home. What little she kept from Nat and Bessie stayed tucked away for her future. It didn't matter much if it were north, south, east, or west;

she just had to get away from her loveless home. Never once did Jenny dream that Thomas entertained romantic notions about her. As far as Jenny was concerned, Thomas was a great friend and a wonderful employer.

As fate would have it, Ms. Chloé took a turn for the worse just days before Jenny's eighteenth birthday. Jenny stayed at her side day and night, singing to her, reading her favorite books, and lavishing her with care. Many evenings Thomas came in to find Jenny and his grandmother fast asleep, their hands still interlocked, as Jenny sat bent over in a chair.

One year after Jenny had begun working for them, Ms. Chloé died. Both Thomas and Jenny were grieved over her passing. Jenny wept as though it were her own grandmother.

"It's something to lose someone and not realize how much they mean to you until they're gone," Jenny told Thomas, her lips trembling as tears coursed down her cheeks.

Thomas held Jenny's hand. It was the first time he had ever had any intentional physical contact with his friend since she had worked for him. While he quietly grieved for his grandmother, his heart ached more for Jenny. Thomas and Jenny sat quietly on the verandah one last time after the island's sole ambulance had taken Ms. Chloé away. There were no books, no talking about his plans, and no reminiscing about her days with Ms. Chloé; it was a time when they both quietly sat together but in separate worlds.

It was Jenny's crackling voice that broke the silence. "It's time for me to move on now, Thomas," she said, her voice barely above a whisper.

Thomas dropped his head and leaned forward, still holding Jenny's petite hands in his. He just nodded his head as she spoke, not wanting to openly display the emotion of yet another loss he was feeling. A tear slipped down his cheek onto Jenny's hand. She had been so caught up in her own grief that she chided herself for being insensitive to Thomas'. Jenny reached over to him and rested her head on his shoulders as her arm wrapped gently around his back. Her tenderness causing him to break down. It was the first time Thomas had shed real tears since his parent's death.

For Thomas, it was a time to say goodbye to his last living relative. There wasn't anyone else he could call his family. He now felt he was again suffering a double blow. It was a poor time for Jenny to leave, he thought. He needed her companionship more than ever before. Truthfully, Thomas never realized how much Jenny meant to him until now. Nevertheless, he knew that she wanted to move away from the island. While he never mentioned it to Jenny, Thomas hated to see her go.

Jenny knew that she cared for Thomas, but thinking of him of anything more than a friend would have been silly on her part. It was not done, and she would be the center of unkind jokes once again in the village. She was just happy for the opportunity to work and save some of her money so that she would someday leave the island for good.

~Chapter Six~

Timing couldn't have been more perfect for Jenny when her older sister Brazella sent for her to live with her on the mainland. That was all the motivation she needed to leave town. She hadn't heard from any of her siblings regularly. Except when they wanted something from the farm to be put on the mail boat.

`"Bloodsuckers!" was all Aunt Bessie had to say about every last one of them. "Instead of them no good chilren tryin' to help you, they sucks all the life out of everything they can," she constantly huffed.

Nothing had really changed since Nat's children moved out. None had ever come back to say thank you or ask if they could possibly do something for their aging aunt and father. Though Aunt Bessie never spoke of it, she had her hopes pinned on Jenny to care for her in her old age. Jenny could work the farm and keep the house for them. For the first time in her life, she saw the value of having Jenny around. All her years of taking care of her brother's daughter would eventually pay off.

It didn't matter so much to Nat. For the time being, he busied himself with his friends, boasting on his strength and virility. He was the youngest man in the settlement to have thirteen living children.

"Yeah," Bessie would retort to his tiresome claims, "it's a pity tho' how all of 'em so useless."

Nat could've said more to his sister's nagging ways, but since she was the only one cooking for him, he bit his lip and refrained from jabbing her about her old dried-up self. Notwithstanding their usual uncomfortable conversations, Jenny managed to inform Aunt Bessie of her sister's request for her to live with them on the mainland. Bessie knew that Brazella couldn't have been sending anything or simply saying howdy. It was typical for her to want somethin'. This time it was Jenny that was sent for. Brazella had taken her demands to another level. She didn't just want the farm produce anymore; she wanted their best farmhand.

As quickly as a lonely tear slipped down Bessie's cheek, she wiped it away with the back of her hand—the same caloused hand used for the last eighteen years to swat the child. Bessie was not one given to soft feelings. Age had crept up and slowed her down a bit. Given that Jenny worked for the Ford's, Bessie didn't bother complaining since the child gave her a regular portion of her money towards their upkeep. With the money Bessie was able to hire an old farmhand from the village to help them out. Her joints had become too painful in the past year to work the field like she did for so many years. Bessie had put on a few extra pounds, and at the moment, her legs were paying the price of her being overweight.

Now she wouldn't have Jenny or her money, and there was nothing she could do about it. The child was too big and fast for her to beat anymore, so there was nothing left to do except to let her have her way.

"If thas what you want, child, ain't nothin' I can do to make you stay, I suppose," she said, looking over her shoulder slightly to see if her meek approach would change her niece's mind.

Jenny was oblivious to her aunt's intended manipulations. Her mind was on the few things she had to pack in the tomato box she picked up from the dock earlier to put her belongings in. She had dreamt of this day for far too long to let anyone try to stop her from taking advantage of this fantastic opportunity.

Bessie clung to the kitchen counter. Her head began to swing, but pride would not let her show any emotion to Jenny. "Well, you better be going child, you know the boat won't wait too long to leave today. They have ta' catch the tide before it gets too low."

"Yes, ma'am." Jenny was beaming as she scooted to her room and tossed her clothes into the box. She didn't think it would be this easy. "Thanks, Aunt Bessie," she said, rushing up to the older lady and giving her a quick hug.

There had never been any affection shared between the two of them, but for some reason, Jenny felt as though she had enough joy, hope, and love in her now to share, even with Aunt Bessie.

In the back of her mind, Bessie hoped that Jenny would return once she met her sister and her good-for-nothin' husband.

With no-one on the island to call a friend or to say good-bye to, except Thomas who was at work on the other side of the island, Jenny quickly made her way to the dock.

Nat Hanna looked up from the deck of his wooden boat as he heard footsteps approaching. He had hoped it was a customer come to buy his fresh catch. There were several other boats at the dock like his hoping to sell their fresh catch. He was sorely disappointed to see who it was.

"What you want, Girl?" he asked, contorting his face as he wiped the beads of sweat from his brow. Nat was still not on good speaking terms with his daughter. "Can't you see I'm busy?"

Not put off by his grunting, Jenny rested the narrow box on her hip and spoke out spunkily to her father.

"Ain't nothin' I want from you, Daddy. I'm eighteen now, and I'm just passin' by to get on the mail boat. You just happen to be here while I was passin', thas all."

Nat was shocked at Jenny, answering him in such a way. She was always so scared to speak up. He often wondered if she could talk at all.

"Now listen to me, you l'il brassy-mouth girl. If you so much as step your foot on that boat, don't look back, 'cause you ain't gat nothin' here for you after that!"

"Humph, I ain't never had nothin' here, so it wouldn't be no lookin' back for me."

Jenny's eyes glassed over for a moment. Nat was fuming. He was unmoved by her emotions. He didn't particularly like the girl, but the thought of her leaving took him by surprise. If she left them now, he would have to pay someone to help the old fella tend to the field; that would be two people on his payroll.

"And what 'bout your aunt?" he roared at his daughter, shaking his fist in her direction. "Did you ever stop to think who gonna look after her when you done gone?" Jenny switched the box to her other hip and pointed her finger at her scowling father completely unaware of the people passing her to go to the mail boat.

"Seems to me, y'all should've thought of that while y'was wailing my backside for no good reason."

By the look in her father's eyes, Jenny knew it was time to quit talking before she embarrassed herself by crying in front of her cantankerous old daddy. More importantly, before he decided to jump up on the dock to give her one last thrashing.

Now that was something he would have liked to boast about with his friends. Nat was getting on in age now, but he was still as brawny as any young blood around town. As Jenny turned to make her way to the mail boat, a customer approached the dock, asking for some fish.

"Move from my boat, Girl," Nat shooed his daughter away like a pesky fly. "And don't let me see your face again."

It was no secret that there was no love shared between the two of them, but somehow, Jenny's heart felt like it was torn out of her and stomped to the ground. It was then she noticed how many people had stopped to listen to their conversation. There was neither comfort nor sympathy shown her, however. Jenny boarded the boat feeling even lonelier than before despite the crowd of people that sat near her.

~Chapter Seven~

J enny waited at the Potter's Cay dock in Nassau for her sister to collect her. Two hours had already passed since she arrived on the mainland, and she was becoming a little restless. All of the other passengers had been long gone. There were no trees around to shade her from the scorching sun, so she sat on a nearby bench next to her box. A young man who had been unloading the boat caught her eye and tipped his hat to her. Jenny turned away. Just as he was making his way toward her, Brazella pulled up in an old half-beat, rust-eaten pale green truck loaded down with her children whose heads were buried deep into large chunks of bright red watermelon.

Smiling at her sister, Brazella honked her horn and waved at Jenny to come. She saw some family resemblance but couldn't figure out why and how her younger sister was so thin when everyone else in the family was big-boned.

"Lawd, it hot out here. Anyway, I reach now so you can toss your l'il box in the back of the truck." Brazella was a husky woman with very little social graces and even less affection. She didn't think twice about being late or not getting out of the vehicle to greet her sister. Her size made getting in and out of the truck an unnecessary discomfort. Jenny could see why the heat would get to her so easily. It was the same way with Aunt Bessie.

"Mind my crabs now, I can't sell 'em if they dead," she shouted outside the window at her younger sister. "Ooh, it's a scorcher today!" she huffed as she grabbed up the hem of her dress to wipe the dripping perspiration from her face.

"Aunt Jenny, can you sit in the back here with us?" asked a pudgy little girl whose face was dripping with watermelon juice.

Jenny looked at her sister, who shrugged her shoulders.

"You might as well. Cause you will be spendin' plenty time with this crew. Anyway," Brazella said, shifting herself behind the driver's wheel to put the truck in gear, "I have'ta pick-up Silas now an' all three of us can't fit in here."

With that, Jenny pranced into the back of the truck and sat on a crate next to the wire coop filled with black crabs.

"Yaay," the little girl squealed as she made her way to sit near her aunt. The other kids were not as eager to make her acquaintance. It seemed like they had more important things on their minds, such as their watermelons.

"So, since you know my name, you think you can tell me yours?" she questioned her niece. The little girl grinned. She had a sweet, lively disposition.

"I'm Janis, but everybody calls me Muffin on account that I remind them of my Grammy." Janis turned and pointed to her siblings. "Now thas' Ike, he's the oldest. He's only thirteen, but he thinks he's a man." Janis held her mouth and giggled, knowing that she had just stirred up a wasp nest with her remarks. "Thas' Gina an' Lena, they twins y'know. Mama say they born on the same day, so the two of them eleven." Muffin pointed to her younger brother who was leaning out of the truck trying to grab hold of the tree branches as they drove past the bushes. "Thas' Samuel, but we call him Sammy, he's seven. Daddy calls him 'big head,' but Sammy don't like that too much, so you should call him Sammy too."

Ike ripped apart his watermelon and stuffed pieces of the skin through the crab cage with one hand and pushed the crabs away from the side of the cage with the other. The crabs weren't at all bothered that they were all heaped up one on top of the other, while huge vacant spaces were available in the cage for their temporary comfort. Jenny tugged on one of Muffin's many plaits.

"Thanks for your introduction. I don't think you told me how old you was though."

Muffin giggled, "Oh, I forgot. I'm nine, but mama says I'm goin' on twenty-nine." She looked at her brother crossly. Ike seemed bent on tormenting their mother's crabs.

Seeing that this was Jenny's first trip to the mainland, she drank in all the sights as Brazella's truck trudged up the bumpy road. The cool breeze on her face was refreshing, considering they had driven away from the harbor into a more congested area of town. There were so many shops and homes and clubs and a whole heap more cars on one road than she had ever seen in her life. Jenny counted almost ten vehicles. Reading about city life was one thing, but seeing it with her own bare eyes was another.

Muffin continued to talk to Jenny, filling her in on the goings-on in the home. Jenny smiled politely but was totally lost in her own thoughts. There were a few familiar sights, she thought, as they drove past large sprawling trees as vendors lined up under them, hoping to sell their wares. Scantily clad children busied themselves behind their mothers, playing hopscotch and shooting marbles in the dirt.

Occasionally, Jenny glimpsed a group of men playing dominoes on a makeshift table under a tamarind tree. Now that sight was the spitting image of what she saw daily back home. The men found unusual ways to repurpose the wooden shipping palettes that were discarded at the dock.

"Back home!" Jenny chided herself. That was the first time she reflected on the island since leaving, and now her mind went and called it home. The truck jerked to a sudden stop in front of a pale blue two-story stone building, jolting Jenny from her thoughts.

A slender lanky man sat sprawled on a rock across the street, his hat pulled down, shading his face as he twirled a toothpick in his mouth.

"Mama, see Daddy there!" Muffin was thrilled to see her father. She almost bolted from the truck to run to him.

"Jus' sit your l'il self down, child, I see him," she rasped, wondering why her husband was across the street and not inside the building working like he was supposed to. Silas got up and approached the truck. It seemed like two strides of his long legs got him across the street in quick time.

"So this is Jenny," Silas drawled flirtatiously at his young sister-in-law, his long white teeth glistening against his shiny jet-black skin. Jenny smiled nervously at her brother-in-law.

"Yes, Suh, I'm Jenny."

Silas tipped his sweat-stained hat and walked around to the driver's side of the truck. "Scoot over, Big Mama," he urged his wife, "your man reach!" Brazella inched her way across the torn vinyl seat, seeming to pout more as she moved farther away.

"What was you doing over there, Silas?" Brazella asked, trying to contain her anger. As usual, Silas played dumb on her, pretending not to hear his wife's question. "Don't tell me you quit again!" Silas continued to ignore his wife despite the escalation of her voice. In the last four years of their marriage, he had changed jobs frequently for some lame reason or another. "I ain't talkin' to myself, y'know!" Brazella twisted her head sharply towards her husband. Silas leaned over and turned the scratchy-sounding radio on. With one swipe of her left hand, Brazella slapped it back off, sending the knob flying to the floor.

"Woman, you gat to learn to control that temper of yours. I will talk to you about this later!"

Later came and went, and finally caught up with Brazella early the next morning while fixing breakfast for the children.

"They laid me off, Brazella," Silas drawled half-heartedly. "Say when biz'ness picks up, they'll come look for me." Brazella spun around and gazed at her husband, who was casually leaning against the kitchen door. "You know the deal, Dumplin'—last to hire, first to fire!" Brazella felt like the wind was knocked out of her.

"But how could they do that? We can't afford to have you stayin' home." Her thoughts went on her sister in the other room. "So what we gonna do about Jenny? We surely can't afford to feed her. Lawd, she'll have'ta pack up and catch the next mail boat back to Daddy."

Jenny couldn't believe what she was hearing. She tapped herself on the head, trying to figure out if this was just a bad dream or somethin'. There was no way she was going back. In truth, if Brazella forced her out to the streets, she couldn't go back. Jenny got up from her makeshift bed on the floor and folded the sheet. She had a plan, and a good one, if only she could get Brazella to agree to it.

~Chapter Eight~

Even if Brazella didn't like the plan, Silas did. Now instead of him slavin' all day, he had both his wife and her sister working to take care of things. Just as Jenny planned, she helped Brazella take care of the home and the children. She found a job doing maid work five days out of the week for Mr. & Mrs. Pinder, and when Brazella needed some time off in the evening, Jenny watched the store for her. Most of Jenny's money went straight into Brazella's hand.

Although Jenny was desperate, she was nobody's fool. She never let on to anyone that she had any money of her own and continued to save a little more every week. Jenny continued her reading when she had time and planned to take a course in typing to better her employment chances. She glanced at the newspaper looking for more favorable jobs and even a place to stay from time to time. Time was definitely drawing nigh for her at her sister's house.

It seemed like it was almost every day she was dodging Silas who seemed intent on setting his grubby hands on her. Why Brazella didn't put a stop to his meandering ways was entirely a mystery. Brazella had walked in on them several times when Silas was making lewd advances toward her little sister. Still, there was no aid or comfort given to Jenny.

Well, enough, was enough! Jenny had her fill of her sister and her husband. They weren't just using her; they were abusing her. She also knew for a fact that Silas' job tried to get him back several times as they had promised. But with Jenny slaving for him, he was living high on the hog. Brazella was no better either. Nowadays, Jenny had to fix breakfast for the children too. Seemed like the only thing Jenny didn't have to do was clean their old beat-up truck. She supposed it was 'cause if clean water hit it, the truck would disintegrate.

Eight months of pouring herself and her money into her sister was sufficient payment for the roof over her head. She was bonding quite rapidly with the children and would be sorry to leave them, but go she must, at the earliest opportunity. Now that she knew how to get around town, she planned on placing more emphasis on finding more skillful employment.

~Chapter Nine~

"**S**o what you good for, Girl?" asked the man across the shop counter.

He continued to busy himself shuffling papers as he spoke, occasionally wiping his sweaty brow with his brawny forearm.

"Well, I can do anything I set my mind to do, Suh, if you give me a chance," Jenny answered the man curtly.

"Humph, thas what they all say. Are y'good with adding?"

"I was the best they had in school!"

The man scratched his head and thought for a moment.

"I suppose you gonna tell me you could read and write too!"

Reaching for the pencil and paper that rested on the counter, Jenny began to inscribe a short poem she remembered. Without another word, she spun the paper around and gave it to the gentleman.

"I'll have to learn you what to do, I guess, but if you want it, you gat the job," he said, squinting to read Jenny's sweeping handwriting.

She grabbed up the paper and folded it neatly on the counter. Jenny was glad she pleaded with Aunt Bessie to do some schooling with the other kids.

"Now," she thought, "it was about to pay off."

The man stretched out his hand across the counter.

"I guess from the look on your face, you'll take the job."

Jenny grinned and clenched the man's hand in agreement.

"Oh yes, Suh," she beamed, "you can bet your bottom dollar, I'll take the job."

"Whas your name, Girl? I think you'll do good here if y'listen. But let me tell you this," he said, pointing his finger toward her. "I don't tolerate no sassy lip, no stealin', and no man hangin' around my shop."

Jenny listened intently.

"Yes Suh, I understan'," and you won't have a bit of problem from me, ever. Oh," she said, remembering his question, "my name is Jennifer Albertha Hanna, but everybody calls me Jenny. Sorry, Suh," she hesitated, "but I didn't get your name, either."

"Hiram Beneby, and you can call me Mr. Beneby."

Mr. Beneby walked toward a nicely dressed colored lady who had just come into the store.

"How do you do today, Mrs. Smith?" he asked the customer courteously. "I see you're back for them tings you asked me to keep for you." Mrs. Smith smiled at Mr. Beneby. She groped through her bag and pulled out a brown envelope.

"There you go, Suh, payment in full. I'll send my boy down in the morning to pick everything up." Mrs. Smith glanced over at Jenny, who had been watching them intently.

"Oh, Mrs. Smith," Mr. Beneby said quietly, "thas my new shop helper. She'll be starting work tomorrow. You can call her Jenny."

Mrs. Smith smiled at Jenny. She knew that she would get along with the young lady.

Jenny waved and sent a big grin toward the lady, "good afternoon, ma'am," she said just before Mrs. Smith turned and left the store. So excited about her new job, Jenny went straight to the Pinder's house to let them know they would be needing a new maid. She thanked them for hiring her and informed them that she wouldn't need the job anymore on account of a new job offer.

"Oh lawdy, lawdy," she said quietly as she walked briskly to the bus stop. "I think I'm gonna bust with excitement!"

Mr. Smith had almost tripled the wages she was earning as a maid for the Pinder's, and now she could afford to rent a room at Ms. Pearline's Boarding house.

"Things are definitely beginning to look up for me," she shouted as she walked out of the boarding house with her very own keys in her hand. Now to sit down with Brazella and share her good news with her sister.

Thinking of her folks on the little island, Jenny lifted her head high and pulled her shoulders back as she remembered how they expected her to fail and come running back home.

"If Aunt Bessie could see me now!" she thought smugly. Truth was Bessie wasn't too particular in seeing Jenny at all, even though the girl sent her a couple of dollars every month to help them get by. She figured Jenny owed her much more on account of her being so kind to her through the years.

None of Nat's other children ever sent money. They only begged for fish and food from the farm. Jenny didn't expect to hear from Aunt Bessie nor her father. She was just content to know they had a couple of dollars in hand since they were getting on in years. They never thought she would amount for much. Nonetheless, Jenny was thankful that they let her finish school.

~Chapter Ten~

Whatever made Jenny think Brazella would be happy for her new accomplishments was quickly wiped from her mind as her sister dealt her a severe tongue-lashing.

"How could you do this to us?" Brazella shrieked, her face appearing to swell even more as she looked for something to throw at her sister. "After all we done did for you, you l'il ingrate!"

Just as she rested her hands on a big black pot to fling at her sister, Silas walked in.

"What you doin', Woman? I could hear your mouth way out in the street." Silas snatched the pot from Brazella's hand. "Big mama, you soon goin' to jail for your temper, mark my words!"

Silas stood between the two women and listened to their tale of what had happened. He looked at Jenny. He was sorry she was going. Actually, he was more than sorry. He was mad. If Jenny didn't stay with them and pay their bills, he would have to find a job again.

"Look, Jenny," he said sweetly, attempting to pacify her. "Come sit down. We could deal with this like adults. You is, after all, a woman now. Whatever the problem is, we can fix it like sensible people."

Jenny shook her head. If she had to walk out without her things, she would do so, but she wasn't planning on staying longer than a few minutes.

"Ain't nothin' more I need to talk about, Silas. I'll just grab my things and leave y'all be."

Brazella held her head and moaned, hoping Silas would move so that she could at least slap her sister side her head.

"Okay," Silas jumped up, not wanting to lose out completely, "get y'stuff, and I'll drop you off to where you're stayin'."

Brazella quickly came to her senses. "Not a day like it," she shouted. "Let her walk or catch the bus. An' hurry up—get out if you goin'! Just to look at you makin' me feel sick. You ain't nothin but a poor excuse for a human being!"

Brazella turned to the pot on the stove with a big spoon in hand. Fussing always made her fiercely hungry, and she plunged into the beans and rice. When her sister came back on her knees beggin' for a place to rest her nappy head, she would deal with her. "And it won't be too much to her liking either," she grunted to herself.

Jenny considered her sister's intervention a blessing. The last thing she wanted was to have Silas showing up on her doorstep and making a complete nuisance of himself. She quickly went inside the room to collect her clothes. It wasn't much more than what she had come with, but it was all she had. When she got her money, she'd give these old rags away. A fresh start deserved a fresh look. Jenny gave Muffin a hug and explained to her and the rest of the kids that she was moving on. None of the kids were happy about her decision and begged her to stay.

"Aunt Jenny, we'll be nicer to you if you stay," Ike said, trying to hold back his tears.

Initially, Ike had been against his aunt moving in with them, but now he had taken to her. She treated him with sense like he was a person with feelings. Although she was not leaving the mainland, he knew he wouldn't be able to see her as he would want to.

"Yeah, and we'll lissen' to you and help you more," chimed in Muffin.

"I'm not leavin' because of anything you children did. You kids are the best. It's jus' time for me to move on." Jenny picked up the little bag with her belongings stuffed inside and said goodbye to the children.

~Chapter Eleven~

The day was quickly passing. Jenny was enjoying her new job as a sales clerk at Hiram's. Mr. Beneby was tough, but fair nonetheless. He showed Jenny what she had to do and then left her to her tasks. Jenny watched intently as Mr. Beneby served his customers politely.

Hiram's was a little dark shop that smelled like kerosene oil and salty sausage. The aisles were narrow, and the shelves stocked high with the basic necessities for the island people. From lard to washboards and hand pumps, Mr. Beneby kept the community supplied. Hiram was pleased with what he had built up over the years.

"The next one is yours, Girl. Let's see what y' gat. And mind you don' run my customers from here."

A while later, a young man walked in. Mr. Beneby had gone to the back of the shop to unpack some new supplies. He watched attentively as Jenny went to assist the customer.

"Good day Suh, welcome to Hiram's. How can I help you?" The girl was good. Beneby was sure he had made the right decision to hire her. She just had to spruce up her looks a bit, and then she'd be jus' all right.

"My mother paid for some stuff yesterday," the young man explained to Jenny, "I'm here to get them." Jenny looked around for Mr. Beneby.

"You can go ahead and give it to him, Jenny," he said, smiling. "That's the stuff right b'side the sack of flour." Jenny walked over to where Mr. Beneby had placed the order.

"There you go," she said, smiling, "they're all yours. And thas your mama's receipt on the top." The young man stooped and picked up several of the boxes off the floor.

"I'll be right back for the others," he assured her.

"Thas okay, I'll help you." Wiping her hands on her dress, Jenny stooped and picked the bag of yellow corn grits and the other bag of rice. "Here you go, Suh," she said to the young man placing the bags in the back trunk of his car. "Thanks for comin', hope to see you again."

Now that she was in the light, he recognized her face. She was the girl he had seen at the dock waiting for her ride.

"Thank you for your help, ma'am. I'm Jimmy." Jenny shook Jimmy's extended hand.

"Good to meet ya, Jimmy, I'm Jenny." Totally oblivious to the sparkle in Jimmy's eyes as he shook her hand, Jenny walked back into the store to attend her duties.

Before she knew it, there were several more customers in the store needing her assistance. Jenny wrote up their orders and packaged their merchandise as though she had been in the business all of her life. Soon it was three o'clock. Her lunch break had come and gone. Mr. Beneby sat in the back of the shop and cut some fresh salami and cheese.

"Come, Jenny," he called to her. "Let's get a quick bite to eat before anyone else comes in." The two of them sat on some stools in the back of the shop, eating fresh salami and cheese with salty crackers.

Every day Jenny's tasks increased, much to her delight. Within a few months, Jenny handled Mr. Beneby's sales, ordered new supplies, and venturing into a minimal amount of bookkeeping. Though a one-stop neighborhood store, Mr. Beneby, under Jenny's advice and taking note of the growing customer demands, started to sell other needful items in his store. Pretty soon, his store became known as a grocery and variety store.

Hiram's sold food, some hardware, fabric, books, and footwear. And because of it, the sales rose incredibly. Six months after being hired at Hiram's, Mr. Beneby increased Jenny's salary by fifty percent. Where Jenny was getting all her fancy ideas to improve the store was unknown to Mr. Beneby, but he was willing to try just about any of her suggestions when he could afford it.

Jenny's latest idea was to put bright lights in the store and paint the inside walls white instead of the faded green that Mr. Beneby admitted having for the past twenty years. He never bothered to paint it because there was so little wall space showing, and you couldn't see it with the low light. Now that Jenny had rearranged the shop a little, it did look more organized. Jenny even coaxed her boss to put in a few chairs for the customers to sit and rest awhile.

"With all the new pretty things you selling, Mr. Beneby, people would be more inclined to shop longer and feel more comfortable, especially if they buying shoes or shopping with chilren."

Beneby knew that was the truth. He had noticed that the older folks spent more time and money in the store when their kids had a place to sit. He was grateful that there was less breakage and children crying on account of the mothers swiping them across their heads for pulling things off the shelf.

"Now Jenny," Mr. Beneby told her firmly when she came with her latest suggestion. Your ideas have been good so far. I would even admit that they have caused the store to bring in more money. But," continued Mr. Beneby while rubbing his nose as though that would help him to express himself better, "I can't see where it makes sense spending unnecessary money on air conditioning!"

Jenny was firm. It was necessary, she thought, for the customers to be comfortable. If not, they would march right over to Harrison's Variety Store, where they got just as reasonable prices but more comfortable with air conditioning.

"Black folks comin' here, Jenny," blared Mr. Beneby. "They ain't shoppin' across to old man Harrison. Ain't I done taught you nothin'?"

Sooner or later, Mr. Beneby would change his mind. Jenny just hoped it would be sooner. He did agree to get rid of the big noisy floor fans and install eight ceiling fans to cool off the place a little better. The only reason he agreed to do that was because the fans were being liquidated from Granger Inn Hotel on account of their renovations. As a matter of fact, Hiram bought out quite a few items from the hotel and made good money by passing the savings on to his customers.

~Chapter Twelve~

J enny stumbled into her room and flung herself across the bed. She was dog-tired. It had been a full day. Before she could rest her weary bones any, there was a knock at her door.

"It's open," Jenny groaned, not wanting to move.

She knew it was probably her new friend and neighbor Gertie. Gertie pushed the door open and briskly strode in.

"Hey girl, what's up?" Jenny sat up on the bed to chat with Gertie for a while.

"I could do with some rest, thas all."

Gertie dragged an old chair from the corner of the room and brought it closer to the bed.

"I had a meeting today with my boss. They say they business is a little slow at the beauty salon, so they lettin' me go. I have to look somewhere else for a job."

Jenny leaned toward the lamp on the side of the bed and turned it on.

"Y'know Gertie, you have a lot of talent fixin' people up and stuff. I think you're gonna do well."

"Thanks, Jen. I knew I could count on your encouragement. But I need your help too." Jenny looked quizzically at her friend.

"Whatever I could do, I'd be happy to help Gertie," she assured her friend.

"You know Manny's Morgue is just across the street from the salon, and they had a "hiring" sign in the window, so I went in to see what it was all about."

"No Gertie, not the place you always laughin' about with your *you kill 'em, we chill 'em* jokes!"

Gertie laughed. "That's the one. Life sure is funny. Anyway, I have an interview with the boss in two days. They need a stylist."

"Well, thas good, ain't you a stylist?" Gertie reached into her bag and pulled out a small camera.

"I am, but I need to show them. I thought if I could take a picture of you before and after, it might help my cause."

"A makeover, eh? Okay, but you owe me big time," Jenny teased her friend.

"Listen, Jen, if I get this job, I promise to give you a free hairdo every week, deal?"

"That ain't necessary, Girl. I'm glad I could help you, though I'm sure I could use some help with my looks."

Gertie positioned Jenny in the chair and took a photograph of her.

"Come, let's get started." Jenny had forgotten that she was tired and followed Gertie to her room for a makeover.

"Girl, do your thing, make me beautiful!"

Gertie laughed at her friend. She was going to get the surprise of her life. After washing the thick grease from Jenny's hair, Gertie dried it and pressed it straight with a hot comb.

"Betcha didn't know your hair was this long, Jen." Gertie placed a small mirror in Jenny's hand to see herself.

"Oowee, Girl—that look like a wig thas so long." Jenny's hair had made it to her shoulder, just past the collar of her blouse.

"I'm gonna cut it in a style to make it even now."

Jenny nodded. She never had a proper haircut before; to tell the truth, she never had it straightened either. Two and a half hours later, Gertie had worked a miracle on Jenny. Her hair was softer and beautiful, and the little make-up Gertie put on her face was a major transformation.

"So, what do you think, Jen?" Gertie prompted her to look in the mirror. A tear slipped from the corner of Jenny's eyes. "Girl, you can't cry now. You'll mess up your make-up, and we'll have to start over again."

Jenny daubed her eyes lightly with a piece of tissue.

"I can hardly believe it's me, Gertie!" She looked in the mirror again. "I think I'll take you up on your offer to help me with my hair. I didn't want to at first," she admitted, grinning. "The thought of you diggin' your fingers up in them dead folks head and then touchin' my hair gave me the creeps."

Both girls laughed.

"Actually, Jen, some of my regular customer's hair was so dirty and smelly, I sometimes wondered if they was dead!"

Gertie took the photograph of Jenny and showed her how to comb her new hairstyle herself. Within minutes Jenny had also learned how to put on a little make-up.

"Gertie, wait for me!" Jenny bolted out of her friend's room, only to come back minutes later with her bag. "I'm going with you. I want you to show me what I need to buy to keep myself looking good."

By nightfall, Jenny bought makeup, hair spray, and a few new inexpensive but fashionable outfits. In a matter of hours, she had dropped the island girl look.

"Girl, you sayin' somethin' now!" Gertie teased her as they ambled back to their rooms. Jenny laid out her clothes for the next day. She didn't even want to wash the stuff off of her face. For the first time in her life, Jenny felt pretty.

When Jenny walked into Hiram's the following day, Mr. Beneby walked up to her, thinking she was a customer.

"Mr. Beneby," Jenny said grinning broadly, "ain't you know this me, Jenny?"

Mr. Beneby's mouth dropped open.

"Jenny, what have you gone and done? You look great, but you look like a whole 'nother person."

All the regular customers had the same response. Some folks came by just to see what everyone was gossiping about.

~Chapter Thirteen~

"Jenny, Jenny," **Gertie shouted** to Jenny before she even got into the guesthouse. "Jenny m'girl I got the job, I got the job."

Jenny opened her door, jumped around with Gertie, quite excited about her friend's success.

"When do you start? Is the pay good? Are the people nice?"

Finally, Gertie calmed down long enough to answer Jenny's questions.

"Can you believe it? Thanks to you, I start tomorrow. And the pay is better than the salon. Seems like not many people take to fiddlin' with dead folks. I suppose you can say most of the people are no bother, on account of them being dead."

Jenny laughed at her friend.

"I guess you'll be comin' home with all kinds of 'dead' jokes soon!"

True to her word, Gertie fixed Jenny's hair for her every week. Jenny was so grateful she began giving her friend a few dollars for her time. Even the men started taking note of the new Ms. Jennifer Hanna. Jenny took a particular fancy for a customer's son, Jimmy Smith, who made her feel special. She wasn't accustomed to the attention she was getting from Jimmy, so it wasn't long before Jimmy started taking Jenny on little outings.

Once in a while, they would just sit by the dock after work and feed the seagulls. When his mother's car was available, Jimmy would stop by the shop to give Jenny a ride home from work. After several weeks of walking on clouds, Mr. Beneby called Jenny into his office. Hiram's Variety continued to blossom, and he saw that Jenny too was beginning to blossom in her own way.

"Sit down, Jenny," he said, motioning to a chair in front of his desk. "I don't mean to get in your biz'ness. Your biz'ness only becomes my biz'ness when it starts to get in the way of your work."

Jenny looked disturbed for a moment. She hoped that she was not out of line.

"You ain't done nothin' wrong, Girl, jus' that you growin' up so quick I don't want to see you gettin' y' feelings hurt. Thas all." Mr. Beneby shifted uncomfortably in his chair.

"I'm glad you care, Mr. Beneby—ain't much people ever cared about me before." Jenny fidgeted with the arm of the chair. "I'll take my time, Suh, and thank you for talkin' with me."

Hiram didn't want to meddle anymore, but he wondered if Jenny knew that Jimmy had been to prison. He knew anyone could change, but the question was, had Jimmy changed?

#

Jenny was seeing Jimmy Smith quite regularly. It was going on two months, and Jimmy wanted to get married. Excitedly, Jenny shared the news with Gertie. She was hoping Gertie would be overjoyed at the prospects of her getting married.

"Girl Jenny, I smell a rat. The man is too much of a sweet talker. He looks like Mr. Clean. He cooks for you, drives you around, takes you to lunch, props you up in front of his family, lives with his ma, and can't keep a job for longer than two weeks."

Jenny rolled her eyes at her friend. "Sounds like you jealous."

Gertie walked towards her friend, "Now, you know better than that. All I'm sayin' is somethin' ain't right here. For all you know, the man could be looking for a cover. Wait, Girl—good things come to those who wait!"

That answer didn't set too well with Jenny. It seemed like she was waiting all of her life for someone just to like her. She didn't figure it was time to be choosy. Gertie wasn't about to press the point further. Her friend was big enough to make decisions for herself. She just was not going to encourage her where she felt she was going wrong. And wrong was the direction she was heading. Although Jenny was angry with her friend initially, she began to watch Jimmy for herself.

Jenny noticed that Mrs. Smith cloaked Jimmy an awful lot. She was always trying to protect him or something. The more time Jenny spent around Jimmy and his family, the more she realized that there was something wrong. Just looking at them sometimes gave her goosebumps. Jimmy seemed to mask his feelings well for a time, but soon, his true personality began to emerge.

"I don't know what's up with this fella, Gertie, but he's beginning to spook me. I've decided to back off for a while." Jenny looked at her friend, thinking she would have a smart reply. "So ain't you gonna say somethin'?"

Gertie shrugged her shoulders. "Seems to me you decided to screw your head back on; it's about time. No decent self-respecting, hard-working girl like you needs to put up with a low-down, good-for-nothin', sweet-talking criminal!"

"Criminal! What are you talkin' about?"

Gertie squinted her eyes at her friend. "How come you're the only person roun' here who don't know that Jimmy jus' get out of jail l'il over two years ago?"

Jenny flopped on the floor in Gertie's room. "Gertie, I jus' moved to the mainland about two years ago!" Jenny felt like she had a blow to the stomach.

Both Jenny and Gertie believed that everyone deserved a second chance to show that they had made a turn for the better. Someone had to give him a chance, or he would be back to his old shenanigans and hanging with the wrong crowd. Gertie just didn't think someone as innocent as Jenny could handle a sweet talker like Jimmy. Jimmy served his time, but no one got the impression that he was remorseful of the events that put him behind bars in the first place. Instead of making sure he was accountable for his actions and on the right track to being a responsible man, Jimmy's mother protected him and stunted his development. She blamed his dysfunction on account of his father's untimely death in his early childhood as well as her inability to nurse him as a baby. Mrs. Smith's guilt did more harm than good for her son.

But that was small things compared to the blow Jimmy's mother felt when the neighbor called her at work some weeks later to let her know about her son's arrest. Seems that an unidentified body of a young girl was found stashed in Mrs. Smith's car trunk. Jimmy had made his move again. This time he tried to bury his mistake. The police found Jimmy digging a hole in his mother's backyard. The neighbors thought it looked suspicious and called the police. Just in time too, Jimmy was about to bury the girl right next to his mother's favorite rose bush.

The thought of spending so much time with Jimmy and not seeing that side of him frightened Jenny. Apparently, this was not the first young girl Jimmy assaulted. It so happened that the third time he was accused of attacking a young lady, his mom was unable to bail him out of his trouble as she had done the first two times. So 'old nasty Jimmy,' as the neighbors called him, was sent to prison for sexually molesting a minor. This time the judge would not be so lenient. Jimmy Smith would spend the rest of his life in prison, or worse.

Jenny felt stupid. The closest people to her had warned her, and she did not take heed. Jimmy was the first man she had taken a hankering to, now she was put off.

"I don't want another boyfriend for as long as I live. I'm going to live alone, just like Aunt Bessie."

Gertie laughed. "That's a bit extreme, isn't it, Jenny? You made a bad choice. Now learn from your mistake an' carry on with life, Girl." Gertie put her arm around her friend's shoulder, "Girl, there's plenty more fish in the sea, and all ain't rotten like the one you pulled up."

Mr. Beneby gave Jenny a few days off to catch herself. "Take some time to rest up now. 'Cause when you come back, I'll be expecting you to work."

Jenny was glad for the time off. She knew she needed to rest, but didn't know-how. All of her life, she busied herself doing one thing or another.

The first day Jenny cleaned her room... several times. She felt boxed in and wanted to escape from her usual environment. That's when she got the idea. The public library—Jenny had been meaning to visit it since she came to town. Now was her chance. When she was younger and wanted to hide away from her daddy and Aunt Bessie, Jenny would grab a book and sit under a tree and read until there was no more light. She always felt like diving into a good book caused her to grow wings and travel the world. Jenny felt exhilarated. She changed her clothes and headed to the library.

~Chapter Fourteen~

Three days in the library, and Jenny felt invigorated. She wanted more of learning, more of life. She felt extremely full. Day after day, Jenny soaked herself in information. She watched students, as well as professional people, come and go. Some people went into a study room off from the main hall. They were smart-looking people, and they talked so good! Jenny felt that's what she needed, to practice speaking properly. Most of them seemed to be well off. At least they came in their own cars.

Even after going back to work, Jenny continued to visit the library. She got to know the staff well and some of the visitors by name. A year later, with the librarians' assistance and a heap of grammar books and audiotapes, Jenny had the command of the English language. In practically three years, Jenny had made great strides in her development. The ordeal with Jimmy was in the past, and her future once again looked bright.

Both Jenny and Gertie had outgrown their rooms at the guesthouse and were figuring on moving. Although they were both making a good salary, neither wanted to put it all into an apartment.

"Why don't we be roomies, Jenny?"

Jenny thought awhile and smiled. It sounded like a good idea. After all, Gertie was her best friend.

"Jus' think, Jen, we could save a few dollars by splitting the rent on a two-bedroom apartment. What do you think?"

"Sounds great to me. Why didn't we think of this before?"

Of course, they both knew the answer to that, but Gertie was gracious enough not to respond.

"I'll meet you at Manny's at 5:30 after I knock off from work, then we can go and check on some apartments."

Gertie nodded. The plan was set. On her way to Hiram's, Jenny picked up a newspaper and scanned the classified ads as the bus cruised along. There was not much to choose from, but she circled the options nonetheless and made a mental note to call the listings on her lunch break.

The day seemed to drag by as Jenny busied herself taking stock of the inventory. Mr. Beneby was out today, paying bills, and left Jenny in charge of the shop and their three new employees. Being totally consumed with her tasks of the day, Jenny not only missed her lunch break but also the opportunity to check on the apartments she had circled.

Later that afternoon, Mr. Beneby returned to close up the shop. As usual, he was pleased with Jenny's accomplishments. He wished he had two of her working for him. Then he wouldn't have to hire the others. The store had grown so much that Mr. Beneby had to take on five employees in the past year. If just one of them was as sharp and willing to work as Jenny, he was sure he would have needed only two of them.

Shortly after five, Jenny sat at the bus stop waiting for her usual ride.

"Which way are you going, Jenny?" Mr. Beneby asked politely.

"Oh, I have to stop off to a friend at the funeral home on West Street today, Mr. Beneby." Mr. Beneby leaned over and pushed his car door open.

"Hop in. I'll give you a ride." In a matter of minutes, Jenny was in front of Manny's Morgue. Driving seemed to save a lot of time. As though he were reading her mind about the convenience of having a car, Mr. Beneby told her that she could have access to the company car as soon as she got her driver's license. He was planning, after all, to purchase a new jet black Plymouth for himself. Jenny could make use of the old one to do the necessary errands for the store and transport herself to and from work.

~Chapter Fifteen~

enny strolled into the funeral parlor. It was near closing time, so she sat in the reception area waiting for Gertie.

"Hey Jen, I'll be done in a few minutes. I jus' have to finish fixin' Ms. Ida's face. Her family jus' left a few minutes ago." Jenny nodded, not wanting to open her mouth lest death slip in through her lips. There was an unpleasant smell in the room which was heavily masked with a floral fragrance.

"I was gonna say take your time, but I changed my mind. Just hurry on up, this place gives me the creeps," Jenny said, rubbing her goose-pimpled arms. "In fact, I think I'll wait outside."

Gertie pulled her friend by the hand toward the chapel.

"Don't be so spooky! It ain't the dead that hurt you, Jen. It's the livin'! Come keep my company while I fix up ole Ida." Reluctantly, Jenny followed her friend into the room. "See here, I had Ms. Ida lookin' so nice, but her family kept grabbin' at her and beggin' her to wake up."

The thought of grabbing a dead body was quite repulsive. Jenny looked away.

"So, how come this box is empty?"

Gertie looked towards her friend. "It won't be for long. Jack Delancey will be fillin' that out tomorrow, soon as the fellas roll him out of the cooler." Jenny edged a little closer to the casket.

"This is so morbid I don't know why I agreed to come in here," Jenny squirmed. Gertie heard the front door open. That was probably Sara. According to the boys who worked in the back, Sara was a faithful visitor to the funeral home for years. Almost every day, Sara came in to pay her respects to the folks that passed. She couldn't read the newspaper to see who died, so she made her rounds to the local parlors to see for herself. Gertie had told Jenny about Sara many times before. Jenny thought someone ought to put a stop to Sara's visits. Sure enough, it was Sara, all dressed in her black from head to toe—moaning just in case she lost someone she knew.

Gertie had an idea. "Jenny," she grabbed her hand and pulled her towards the empty box. "Thas' Sara comin' in."

"So!" Jenny pulled her hand away from Gertie. Her friend continued to press her point, mischief spreading all over her face.

"So, now we can scare the daylights out of Sara and put a stop to these visits altogether."

Not convinced that what her friend wanted to do was a good idea, Jenny squinted her face at her friend.

"I got the picture, Gert, but wild horses couldn't get me in that box."

Gertie didn't give up easily; "Would fifty dollars get you in?" she prodded.

Jenny tossed her handbag to the side and puffed the silky pillow she was about to lay her head on.

"Which way do I put my feet?" She asked her friend, matter-of-factly. As quick as a flash, Jenny jumped into the box and laid herself off like a corpse. Gert wiped Jenny's face with powder, then raced behind the door to view Sara in action.

Sara stopped at the first corpse. She didn't recognize the lady at all. But that didn't stop her from inspecting her and even holding a little conversation. Tiptoeing like a royal prima donna from a bad movie, Sara held up her white handkerchief, waving it gently in the air as she moved to the next casket. Again, she did not recognize the gentleman. Sara turned the man's face towards her and, with her gloved hand, pried his mouth open to see his teeth.

Gertie could hardly contain herself. She covered her mouth to squelch the laughter that was bubbling inside of her. Tears welled in her eyes, her shoulders shook uncontrollably. Sara moved over to Jenny, who was in the casket on the other side of the room. Jenny had watched Sara's every move from the moment she stepped into the room. If Sara was thinking of putting that glove on her, she had better think twice.

Sara leaned over the coffin.

"This a scrawny l'il one, and she's young, too." Sara started to cry. She took her little hanky and blotted her eyes. "Oh, I wish you didn't have to die so young, Child," she moaned. "Oh, lawdy, oh lawdy, why it had to be you and not me?"

Gertie's body shook with laughter. Sara said the same thing to anyone she thought was younger than forty. Gertie's feet slid slightly from under her. Her hair was caught on the light switch which sent a humming surge through the room.

For a split second, the light flickered off and then back on. Gertie couldn't have planned it any better. Sara stopped crying for a second and looked around the room. Noticing that Jenny's make-up had smeared on her face slightly, she spat on her glove to fix it. Just as she was about to clean the smudged lipstick by Jenny's mouth with the damp glove, Jenny opened her eyes and grabbed Sarah's hand, pushing it away from her. Gertie thought she would die from laughter as Jenny sat up in the coffin. Not realizing that it was a prank, Sara belted a high-pitched scream and collapsed to the floor.

"Oh Lord, Gertie, we done killed the woman," Jenny whispered, petrified of what she had done as she climbed from the casket.

Gertie was still laughing so much that tears drained down her face. "Gertie, this ain't funny no more. What are we going to do?"

Gertie walked over to a cabinet for some smelling salts, still bent over with laughter. She couldn't have done a better job herself. Jenny composed herself and put Sara's wig back on her head as Gertie placed the smelling salts to the old lady's nostril. In no time, Sara was up on her feet. She looked at Jenny and Gertie and ran out of the funeral home as fast as she could, supposing she had seen a ghost. That triggered Gertie's cackling once more.

"Gertie," Jenny shouted at her friend. "It ain't that funny. We could've frightened her to death." Gertie wasn't bothered.

"No fool, she could've burned you with that old sour spit," Gertie squawked, holding her side as she attempted to contain the laughter. "Listen, the only way Sara would have died in here would have been by drownin'," she noted. Jenny didn't understand. "Well, if I hadn't put the salts to her head when I did, she would have drowned right there where you're standing." Gertie pointed to the puddle her friend was standing in.

"Oh, gross! Now I really feel sorry for her. I don't know why I let you talk me into this."

There were no visits to the funeral home from Sara from that time on. When asked by the staff why she didn't visit them anymore, Sara merely contorted her lip, squinched her eyes at them, and replied, "The time has not come for me to reveal the mysterious goings-on in that place."

Eventually, Gertie calmed down enough to talk to Jenny without bursting into laughter as she recalled the vivid sights at the funeral home. Since then, Jenny refused to meet Gertie there again. She didn't even want to be seen in the area, in case she bumped into Sara.

~Chapter Sixteen~

I t was July 3, 1981, when Jenny got news that her father was ailing. Her sisters and brother thought she should return to the Island to look after him, but Jenny was adamant that she was not going back.

She had been on the mainland for about two years, and not one of them had reached out to her. Now they were telling her to go back to Maruba to care for a man who openly despised her.

When Ike heard about the situation, he volunteered to live with his grandfather and look after him, which suited all the siblings well. Tending to their old pa was an inconvenience none of them wanted to commit to. Since Ike wanted a change from living on the mainland, he jumped at the opportunity to move away from his quarrelsome parents. Nat was much along in years now, having outlived his sister Bessie who passed away exactly a year and a half before. He was looking good, considering he was just shy of seventy-eight years.

After Bessie had died, Nat hadn't been making much of an effort to take care of himself. When his neighbors called Brazella to inform her of Nat's condition, he was fiercely angry. His children didn't check on him much since their mother passed, and he wasn't interested in them now.

"I don't want them vultures swarmin' aroun' me, waitin' for death to suck me into the grave," he told his friends. The only child who consistently sent mail to him was Jenny. He knew she had sent some to Bessie before she died, but now she had begun to send them to her daddy. Nat was never interested in what she might have to say, so he never opened the letters. He figured he'd get to them just when he felt good and ready, if ever.

Well, a good while passed, and Nat still didn't feel like it. The letters stayed piled high on Bessie's bed, untouched. Every month Nat walked into the room when the mail had come and tossed the envelope on the bed. Now that Ike had moved into Bessie's room he was curious to see what his Aunt Jenny had to say month after month.

Ike pried open the first envelope. It was just a blank piece of paper his aunt had used to conceal the money she had sent. He went through some others; it was the same thing, just money. Ike looked around the old house. It was in bad shape. His grandfather was looking gaunt and tired, not having much money to feed himself, although he could rustle up a few coins for a drink. Even so, he had about 17 envelopes, including several addressed to Bessie stashed on a bed in his house, catching dust.

Nat sat on the porch enjoying the cool evening breeze. Ike strode over to him with an enormous grin plastered on his face. He had taken to the boy. He reminded him much of himself when he was young. Tall, strapping, and willing to take on the world, Ike waved the familiar envelope in front of his grandfather's face.

"You'll never guess what I've found, Grampa." Nat looked up at Ike and smiled.

"What y'got there, Son?" he humored him.

Ike poured the contents of the letter on Nat's lap.

"Grampa, there's lots more where that came from," he told him proudly.

Nat grimaced. He didn't know if he should be angry with Ike for opening his letters or with himself for not opening them.

"How much you gat in there, Boy?" he asked Ike, trying to conceal all excitement.

"I ain't added all up yet, Grampa, but it's more than enough to fix this leaky roof and do most of the other things that needs to be done around here.

"You don't say!" Nat pursed his lips, not bothering to hide his enthusiasm this time. "Tell y' what, you run down to Passion Bar and bring me a bottle of their best liquor, and we'll celebrate." Ike shook his head and smiled at his grandfather.

"Good try, Gramps, but you know the doctor's orders, you can't drink no more."

"Thas' right, Boy. I ain't drinking no more. But I ain't gonna drink no less either."

Ike smiled at his grampa; he always had somethin' witty to say. It was hard to believe the stories his mama and aunties told him about Gramps. He sure had softened up over the years.

"Tomorrow, Grampa, I'll start getting this old house back on its feet."

That was precisely what Ike did. For the next several weeks, Ike worked hard and long, repairing the roof, floorboards, windows, rails, and general fixing in the house. Nat's house was the talk of the town. Ike had put a fresh coat of green paint on it and trimmed it white. Ike claimed his next venture was to get the farm back in order. He felt they should at least be able to feed themselves a little better from the land since Nat had stopped his fishing.

Nat was proud of the boy. He told him so, many times. Ike was quick to mention that it wouldn't have been possible without Jenny's money. That, of course, was the truth, but Nat didn't care to discuss it further. He certainly wasn't going to call her or drop her a note, as Ike suggested.

"You wouldn't understand, Boy," he told his grandson. "It just won't be a manly thing to do."

Two months later, Nat Hanna passed away. Ike had him buried next to his sister Bessie in the public graveyard. Ike had called his mother weeks before and told her to inform the family that Nat was low, but no one seemed to be able to make it up for a visit, nor for the funeral. He did get a letter from his family on several occasions, inquiring into their father's will.

Ike searched the box where Nat kept his important papers. Sure enough, in the box was a little note he painfully scribbled only days before his passing. Nat left the house and property to Jenny, his loveless child. Just in the event his other children tried to weasel it away from her, Nat had his doctor sign the paper as a witness. Ike read the letter Nat had written to Jenny and wept. He was touched by Nat's sincerity and knew it took everything his old grampa had left in him to write the letter.

Several weeks after the funeral, another envelope came from Jenny; this time, a letter accompanied the money. Jenny reached out to her aging father as though the past had never happened. She wanted to come to visit him and wondered if he would receive her. Ike realized then that his mom had not informed Jenny of her father's death.

~Chapter Seventeen~

The mail boat pulled into the tiny dock behind the village stores. Not much had changed since she left several years before. Surprisingly, there was no trace of the bitterness Jenny thought she would have had returning to her childhood home. She stepped onto the rickety dock dressed in a white cotton halter top and a pair of pink and white pedal pushers slacks with her favorite pair of white sweet water lace-ups. Jenny looked around for her father's boat as she held on to her white wide-brimmed straw hat, half expecting to see him peddling his wares to impatient customers.

Jenny thanked the young man for her luggage and walked toward the road, hoping to see a familiar face. Several years ago, Jenny walked the same dock, clutching a box with all of her worldly possessions, not once desiring to return to the little island. Today, she walked confidently, no longer a little girl eager to run away from home but a young lady who was willing to forgive the past and embrace the future.

The corner pump still remained across from the shops. Jenny smiled as she remembered the days she and Blake Smith had tussled over the ground for one thing or another. A young man pulled up in front of her in an old car.

"You need a taxi, Ma'am?" he asked politely, not recognizing who she was.

Blake hadn't changed a bit. He was still big and chubby, hardly able to get out of his own way. His pants were torn and scuffed up like he had just come from a fight or the fields. Jenny walked towards the car. Taxi was sprawled across the door with aqua house paint, just in case you missed the little plastic sign on the roof. Jenny smiled at Blake and nodded. He still had not recognized her.

"This your first trip on the island, Ma'am?" he asked as he climbed into the driver's seat.

"No, actually, it isn't," Jenny answered him with her new polished talk.

"Oh well, I don't ever remember seeing you round here, Ma'am." She just couldn't keep her identity from Blake any longer.

"Blake, for as many times as I whupped your tail at the pump, you should be able to recognize me!"

Blake swung around to face Jenny. He pulled his car to the side of the road.

"Naw," he was visibly stunned. "You can't be... Jenny Hanna?"

Jenny put her fists in his face playfully, "I can't be, huh? Should I prove it, Blake?" Blake looked Jenny over; he couldn't believe his eyes.

"Jenny, but you sound so different, and you look so pretty too!" Jenny laughed. It felt good to be one up on Blake again.

"No hard feelings, hey, Jenny? I mean we was jus' kids havin' some fun and stuff." Still laughing at her old childhood tormentor, Jenny reached out to shake Blake's hand.

"I'd say it's time we called a truce."

"Truce," Blake took hold of her hand, shaking it lightly.

#

Ike ran from the field when he saw Jenny walking towards the house. She looked around, quite happy that the house had been kept up so well. Resting her luggage on the bottom step, she turned and watched Blake drive down the road. She wondered where her father could be. He must have expected her, as she had written almost a month before.

"Unless," she thought, "he still didn't want to see her again."

"Aunt Jenny, Aunt Jenny," Ike shouted happy to see his aunt. "I was supposed to meet you at the dock, but time jus' ran away from me, I guess." Jenny hugged her nephew.

"That's alright, Ike. I'm happy to see you're keeping yourself busy. This place looks marvelous!"

Ike beamed with pride.

"I couldn't have done it without your help, Aunt Jen," he said, looking proudly at his handy work.

"Come inside. I made some cool lemonade for you." Ike picked up Jenny's bags and took them into the house. Jenny flopped onto an old chair by the window. "Aunt Jen, I'm glad you're here. We've got to talk. It's about Grampa." Jenny sat up slowly.

"Where is he, Ike? I guess I half expected to see him sitting on the porch."

Ike smiled. "Well, that was his favorite spot in the whole house."

Totally oblivious to Ike's using the past tense to speak of her father, Jenny inquired further.

"So where is he, Ike? I thought he would have put the past behind him." She got up and peered out the window. "Well, no matter, you take me to him. He'll have to face up to me sooner or later."

Ike dropped his head and stuffed his hands nervously into his pockets.

"What's the matter, Ike? You look like you've lost your best friend." Ike looked up at his aunt, his eyes welling with tears.

"I thought you got the message, Aunt Jen. Grampa died last month." Jenny closed her eyes and held her forehead. She couldn't believe what she was hearing. Nat was gone, and she didn't get a chance to say goodbye.

"I just wanted to let him know that I've forgiven him for the way he and Aunt Bessie treated me," she whispered, wiping a stray tear from her eye. "I understand now what it must have been like to have Mama die and to be saddled with an infant. It wasn't right, but I forgave him. It took all these years, but I can honestly say that I've forgiven him." Ike walked to the table and picked up the letter he had left there for Jenny to see.

"Aunt Jen, Grampa knew that you forgave him." Ike scratched his head, not being accustomed to consoling anyone. "He wasn't good at saying what he felt unless it was somethin' out of the way— if you know what I mean." Jenny smiled at her nephew. Ike was trying his best to mend her daddy's broken fences of the past. "I'm not just sayin' all this to make you feel better, Aunt Jen. Here, read this for yourself." Ike passed the letter to his aunt.

"Jenny," it read scrawled across the yellowed page. "I shoulda dun betta by you, gurl. I ain't purfect, no one is. I jus' hope you forgive a ole fool like me. You fiery jus like ya ma, an' ya look a l'il somethin' like her too. Every time I saw you I membered I ain't had Muffin no more an' it broke ma heart. I want you to keep this house. You wuz born here and your ma tole Bessie you was a special blessin' when you was born. I was too bline to see that 'til now." The scrawly note was signed, "Your daddy, Nat Hanna."

"Here, Aunt Jen, wipe your face." Ike handed her a piece of tissue. Her make-up had melted and drained down her face as she wept while reading her father's letter.

"I must look like a silly owl, huh Ike." Ike smiled back at his aunt and squeezed her hand.

"Somethin' like that, but I won't tell no-one."

After Ike's cold glass of lemonade and a bologna sandwich, Jenny strolled down to the graveyard to pay her respects to her father and her aunt.

-

~Chapter Eighteen~

A cool breeze wisped past Jenny's face as she ambled up the winding path towards Thomas' house. She stopped for a moment and caught her breath, wiping the perspiration from her neck. The trek seemed longer than she remembered. Jenny smiled to herself. Perhaps it was just her level of desperation that erased the thought of toil as she climbed the hill to work every day.

The house stood majestically on the hill. It was a beautiful sight. Thomas had painted the old colonial structure a cheery yellow with white trim. The wrap-around porch, with its distinctive rails and rows of French doors, made Jenny stop and smile. How peaceful, she thought, as she continued to make her way up the path. Before she could knock on the door, it quickly swung open, almost causing her to topple backward.

"Oh, I'm sorry," the young lady who had opened the door apologized. Jenny had never seen her before and wondered if Thomas had gotten married. Her accent seemed quite different. Jenny wondered if she were from France or one of those fancy European countries she read about many times. "What can I do for you?" the lady continued, her long blonde hair falling on her face. She looked Jenny up and down, not sure what she had come for.

"I'm here to see Mr. Ford," Jenny stated matter-of-factly.

"Then, Dear, you have come to the wrong door. Helpers enter through the kitchen."

Just as Jenny was about to turn and leave, Thomas called from inside.

"Marianne, who are you talking to out there?" Marianne swirled her ginger ale in her glass and closed the door as Jenny returned to the path.

"No-one, Cherié. It's not important. She's leaving now!" she shouted down the passageway.

Thomas spotted Jenny as she was making her way back down the path. She was surprised that Thomas would marry such an unmannerly person.

"Excuse me," he said, following behind Jenny. "I'm sorry that Marianne has scared you away. How can I help you?" Jenny turned to face her former employer.

"Mr. Ford, you probably don't remember me, but I..." before Jenny could say another word, Thomas recognized her.

"I don't believe my eyes. Jenny—Jenny Hanna—it's so good to see you. Please, please come inside." Jenny hesitated, smiling politely at Thomas, "I don't think that's such a great idea." Thomas shook his head.

"Oh, Marianne was just leaving. She's my decorator. Marianne has been such a help getting the old house looking spritely again that she sometimes goes overboard, thinking that she is the Madame of the house."

Jenny turned politely towards the path again.

"I didn't intend to intrude, Mr. Ford. I'm just in town for a few days and thought I'd stop in to see how you were doing."

Thomas looked up at the house and then back at Jenny. He had missed her and didn't want to risk not seeing her before he, too, went away on a business trip.

"Jenny, it's still Thomas, not Mr. Ford, you know." Thomas quickly skirted in front of her attempting to block her path. "Are you staying at your home in the village?" Jenny nodded, feeling embarrassed and wanting to leave quickly. "So sorry to hear that your father died."

"Thank you, that's kind of you to say. But I must be going now."

Jenny somehow felt a little disappointed in their meeting. How silly, she thought, for her to have any expectations at all. Thomas persisted nonetheless.

"An old classmate of mine is in town, Jenny. He'll be stopping by later this evening for dinner. I would love it if you would come back and join us. I can collect you at say...six o'clock."

Thomas turned his face to the side, smiling—almost pleading with her.

"Okay," Jenny answered coyly, unable to resist meeting up with her old friend again, "six o'clock is fine."

"Great!" Thomas answered excitedly. He felt like a young boy again as he walked up the hill backward not wanting to lose sight of her. "I'll be looking forward to seeing you then."

Thomas watched Jenny walk down the path until she was out of sight. He hoped he hadn't made a fool of himself, but he just had never met anyone quite like Jenny before. She simply wasn't just the lovely person he used to enjoy being with. Jenny had undergone a transformation— she was breathtaking!

~Chapter Nineteen~

Before she knew it, six o'clock was upon her. Jenny finished putting on the final touches of her make-up when she heard Thomas' car drive up in the yard. Just as Ike was about to call his aunt, she stepped from her room in an attractive yellow and white floral cap sleeve cotton dress that made her look like a million dollars.

"Oowee," he shrieked, teasing his young aunt. "I think I'd better get dressed and be going with you." Jenny laughed at her nephew and twirled in the living area before walking out the door.

"I take it you approve, Ike?" Ike was speechless. He could only nod his head and smile.

Thanks to Gertie, Jenny had a new look and a matching wardrobe. It was good to feel attractive. It sure was better than being called "bubba lips," as some children called her in school. Thomas stood with his mouth somewhat agape as Jenny greeted him. "Lovely" was not a fitting word for Jenny tonight. She was simply stunning.

"It's a beautiful night out, isn't it, Thomas?" Jenny stood on the porch, looking into the sky and breathing in her fill of fresh island air. Thomas had still not taken his eyes off of Jenny.

"Beautiful," he mumbled, feeling somewhat clumsy.

Not entirely comfortable herself, Jenny continued to talk about the weather. As they drove up the hill into the carport, Jenny noticed a slender young man with blonde hair sitting on the verandah fiddling with a camera. He immediately stood up as Jenny and Thomas approached.

"I can see why you wanted me to stay and hold down the fort, my friend," the young man grinned at Thomas. "I probably would have done the same thing had I such a gem."

"Jenny, this is my former classmate, Eric Journier. Eric, this is Jenny." Eric beamed.

"Enchanté, Mademoiselle," he greeted her with his melodious accent. "My friend was wise not to tell me about your beauty, or I would have come prepared with my whole studio."

"Eric is a famous fashion photographer, Jenny. He has a keen eye for beauty, so watch out for him. He has no shame."

"It's so good to meet you, Eric. I think I have heard your name mentioned before."

The truth was, anyone who read the latest fashion journals had heard about Eric Journier. He was a jet setter, an excellent photographer, and almost always had a beautiful girl clinging to his arm.

"Jenny, can I get you something cool to drink? I had some lemonade chilling in the refrigerator, especially for you. I remembered you always loved to have a tall glass every day."

"Thank you, Thomas that sounds delightful. You sure have a great memory."

As soon as Thomas withdrew to the bar for their drinks, Eric made himself more comfortable with Jenny. He was quite charming and funny too. Jenny could see how he managed to turn the ladies' heads. In no time, Eric had Jenny so relaxed and laughing at his stories that she hardly noticed his snapping photos of her.

"He's a crafty one, Jenny, don't believe a word he says," Thomas interrupted, resting a tray of hors d'oeuvres on the table in front of them.

"I believe you, Thomas, but he's such a great storyteller, even though he has probably enlarged the story tremendously."

The evening was lovely. Thomas and Eric's tall tales of each other seemed to stretch beyond reason. Jenny couldn't remember ever laughing so much. She hadn't seen Thomas in this way before. She loved his sense of humor or dry wit and charm, as Eric noted when sharing their escapades in school. Eric looked at his watch. It was well past eight o'clock, he had a long drive ahead of him and would need to eat soon. Time had flown.

~Chapter Twenty~

After dinner, Eric sat on the oversized sofa next to Jenny. His countenance was serious now.

"Jenny, I'd like you to consider accompanying me on my next shoot in Madrid, Spain. You're a natural. Quite frankly, I think you could very well be our next cover girl." Eric paused and looked at Jenny's hands, checking for a wedding ring. "That is unless you don't have a husband and kids waiting home for you."

Thomas was also interested in her answer. He didn't stop to ask her if she was married and hoped she wasn't. He also knew his friend Eric and his reputation for having a long line of models falling for him.

"No, I'm not married, Eric." Jenny knew that Eric was serious, but she couldn't help but see the humor in the whole conversation. "And I really don't think I'm model material. You do want the magazines to sell, don't you?"

"Listen, Jenny, think about it. All of your expenses will be taken care of. It's a great opportunity to travel and see the world. You'll have your own apartment, and if you don't like it, you are not obligated to go on any other shoot." Eric was quite persuasive.

"I can't just leave my job like that, Eric. I'll have nothing to come back to," she rationalized.

"My dear Jenny, it's entirely up to you. You have to decide. But I'll tell you this—you will probably earn more than your annual salary in one photo shoot."

Thomas could not help but overhear their conversation. He knew what Eric said was true. He also knew that an opportunity like this one might not pass by again. Jenny looked at Thomas, searching his eyes for his opinion.

"Well, Thomas, what do you think?"

Thomas ran his fingers through his thick black hair and sat on the piano stool. "Jenny, everything he is telling you is true. The bottom line is: only you can decide if this is what you want for yourself or not."

Eric looked at his watch again and stood up. He hated to leave them, but an early morning awaited him. He needed to be refreshed for the shoot at Thomas' property in the morning. Thomas had arranged for Eric to stop over with a few models to help promote the new upscale boutique at the resort.

"Think about it, Jenny. I'll be leaving for Madrid the day after tomorrow. You can give me your final word by then." He leaned over and kissed Jenny on the cheek, "whatever your decision, it was great meeting you, and I hope to see you again soon."

Thomas walked his friend towards the door, thanking him for his visit.

"Oh, Jenny," he said, turning towards her, "should you decide, the shoot starts in late May. I'll forward you the contract and an advance."

This must have been a dream. Jenny couldn't believe this was happening to her. The odd thing about the whole event was that she never saw herself as a model.

Thomas walked towards the sofa pensively. He knew that Jenny would be returning to the mainland in a few days. He didn't want her to leave the island at all.

"Why so glum, Thomas?" Jenny quizzed him. They had such a lovely evening she couldn't imagine him looking out of sorts.

"I'm just sorry that you have to leave again. I haven't felt this vital since, since..." Thomas stopped short in his sentence, he didn't want to expose his heart and risk pushing her away. Jenny reached over and took Thomas' hand. The last time she held his hand, it was to comfort him at his grandmother's funeral.

"Since your parents were alive, Thomas?" she attempted to complete his sentence.

"No, Jenny, since you were last here." Thomas placed his hand on top of hers and gently squeezed it.

Complete shock must have registered over Jenny's face. She never dreamed Thomas had any such thoughts towards her.

"I'm sorry if I made you feel uncomfortable, Jenny. I wanted to be honest. I didn't want you to leave again without your knowing what you really meant to me."

Jenny smiled nervously at Thomas. Quite honestly, she wouldn't let herself think of Thomas in that light. Their differences were considerably obvious, and she couldn't justify extending herself to open rejection. The night seemed to have come to an abrupt end for Thomas. He threw his head back on the sofa, wondering if he had just shot himself in the foot.

"You just caught me off guard, Thomas. I would have never imagined that I would be in your thoughts at all."

Thomas shook his head. "Jen, you underestimate yourself. Surely you must have had an idea how I felt about you." He sat to the edge of the sofa, attempting to convince her of where his heart has always been. "I looked forward to those evenings you stayed late to read to my grandmother."

Jenny knew they enjoyed each other's company. She also knew that she was happier with the Fords than with anyone else in her entire life. But even that didn't matter. Her reality was in the village with her daddy and Aunt Bessie. For that reason, her heart was set on leaving the island, not getting involved in a relationship that could not go anywhere.

"I tried seeing other girls, Jen, but it never worked out. My time with them never measured up to our time together. I even considered going to the mainland to see you but decided against it. I decided just to keep myself busy with my work."

Thomas got up from the sofa and strode toward the porch door. Leaning against the open frame, a cool breeze swept past his face as he gazed down the bushy hillside. He quietly reminisced on the many evenings they had spent on the porch. Back then, Thomas was not as open with his feelings toward Jenny as he would have liked. He turned to look at Jenny. He believed that they had something special even if she did not realize it. Thomas wasn't bothered by her inability to speak, he figured the cat was out the box, and there was no turning back.

"Our times together back then, Jen, was the highlight of my days." Jenny got up and placed her glass on the table.

"Thomas, why didn't you say anything?" she queried as she walked toward the door. She could feel the intensity of his words. Jenny's heart fluttered, sending cool shivers down her spine. She leaned on the door across from Thomas, not wanting to get too close in the event he sensed the effect he was having on her.

"You wanted to go away, Jenny—to get away from this place and everyone in it. I figured I was part of that lot. I wasn't thinking clearly, I guess, with my grandmother having just passed. In retrospect, Jenny, I guess I was just too indecisive. I didn't think you would want to stay since all the gossip had started about you and me."

That was news to Jenny. "What gossip? I wasn't aware of anything being said," she quickly composed herself.

"It seems like the whole village knew how I felt about you." Jenny walked gingerly over to where Thomas stood.

"If they gossiped then," she declared heartily, "I guess they'll have a field day of talks tomorrow." Thomas wasn't quite sure what Jenny meant.

"Why would they talk tomorrow?"

"Well, aren't you going to show me your beautiful resort tomorrow? I've heard you talk about it for so long it would be a shame to come all this way, only to turn back because of wagging tongues."

Thomas agreed wholeheartedly. He was thrilled that Jenny had still planned on accompanying him to South Point Resort. Apparently, he had not frightened her away completely. Thomas did his best to suppress his desire to pull her closer to him. He swirled the fast-melting ice in his glass and drank the last of his beverage. Jenny blushed nervously. In the heat of the moment, she was within inches of Thomas' face. She froze, not knowing quite what to do, though she wished he would do something.

"I think I'd better get you home, Jen. It's getting late." Jenny nodded, somewhat disappointed that Thomas had not embraced her. He took her hand, kissed it, and held it to his cheek for a moment. "I'm glad you decided to come with me tomorrow, Jen."

Jenny was sure that Thomas could hear her heartbeat as it thumped uncontrollably through her skin.

"Yes, Thomas," she whispered, wanting him to pull her close to him, "I'm glad also."

~Chapter Twenty-one~

It seemed like Jenny had not slept a wink at all. She came home way past midnight. Thomas had mesmerized her beyond her imagination. Their time together reminded her of their friendship several years ago, except this time, there seemed to be boundless fireworks alight. Jenny's mind raced, rehashing every word Thomas had spoken to her. Unable to sleep, Jenny paced the floor, trying to make sense of what she was feeling, wondering what it would have been like if he did kiss her.

She laughed to herself, thinking that she might have fainted or just embarrassed herself entirely since she didn't know the first thing about kissing. But something inside her wanted Thomas to hold her and never let her go.

By two a.m. Jenny was sure that she had remembered Thomas' gestures, his smile, the way he sat, the long dark hair on his arms, his fragrance...whatever had slipped past her in their earlier days stood out clearly—yet sweetly. Jenny remembered his kindness, his rugged good looks, and his fit body. Thomas was solid but lean; it was apparent that he kept himself physically fit.

One thing Jenny remembered about Thomas was his dedication to his work. Now after meeting his schoolmate Eric, she saw his commitment to his friends along with an adorable sense of humor...Jenny held her face to keep from smiling; the ongoing surge she felt was like refreshing waves of love.

Jenny quickly dodged that thought. The last thing she needed to do was to make the situation more than it was. After all, she didn't even know what it felt like to be in love. But it did feel as though someone was blowing a cool, refreshing breeze into her parched soul.

An hour or so after Jenny had finally drifted off to sleep, Ike got up to look after his crops. When he returned several hours later, Jenny was up, dressed, and preparing breakfast.

"I thought I smelled somethin' cookin'. I didn't think you would be up so early this morning, Aunt Jen. You hardly slept all night!" Ike looked at his aunt. She looked different. He had never seen her looking so happy. "Aunt Jen," he pressed, "mind tellin' me why you look as though your feet ain't touchin' the floor when you walk?"

He also noticed that she couldn't stop smiling, but he dare not mention that too. If anyone deserved to be happy, it was his aunt. Ike went to the kitchen sink to wash his hands while still mischievously grinning at Jenny.

"You're a freshy, aren't you, Mister?"

Jenny threw a small potato playfully at Ike. She enjoyed his company. Having Ike in the house was a huge difference from the tense atmosphere she grew up in. In all of her years of living in the house, Jenny never remembered the sense of calm quite like now. She had given the house some thought and felt it a good time to find out from Ike what his plans were. Setting his breakfast on the table next to her, Jenny motioned to Ike to sit and eat.

"Ike, have you decided what you want to do now that your grandpa has passed?"

Ike nodded. He had thought of staying on but didn't quite know what his aunt wanted to do with the house.

"If you stayed, what do you plan on doing?"

"I'm pretty handy at building and fixin' stuff. Since I fixed up this house, people have been offering me jobs all over the place."

Impressed with the upgrades, especially the indoor plumbing, Jenny could see why her nephew was in high demand.

"Ike, as long as you would like to stay here, you may. So long as you work, look after the property, and in two years, consider taking some classes to further your education."

Ike shrugged his shoulders as he stuffed a spoonful of scrambled eggs and yellow grits into his mouth.

"I don't know about the schoolin' part, but like you say, I could give it some thought."

Jenny got up from the table and kissed her nephew on his head. She was glad he was there at the old homestead.

"There are some ground rules, though, Ike. We'll get to them later. In the meantime, I have to finish getting ready. Thomas will be here any minute."

Ike grinned, but he dared not to say a word. He had wondered why his aunt was floating. He heard the answer to his question drive up in the yard.

"Bye, Sweetie," she said, kissing Ike on his forehead as she walked out the door past him.

"You enjoy yourself, Aunt Jen," he said as he waved to Thomas, who was making his way around the car to open the door for Jenny.

"Good morning, Jenny. Did you sleep well?" Thomas asked politely.

"When I did manage to doze off, it was quite restful, thanks."

Thomas shut the door behind Jenny and got into the driver's seat. He seemed to drink in her presence before turning the ignition to start the car.

"How was your night, Thomas? You look well rested?"

"I'm fine. Thank you for asking."

Thomas hardly slept the whole night. He sat on the verandah for several hours, thinking about Jenny and some important decisions he had to make.

Jenny had never really paid much attention to Thomas' looks before last night. She knew he was attractive, but now she could hardly take her eyes off of him. The way the sun caused his black hair to gleam and, oh, the gentle smile lines around his mouth. Thomas' presence exuded strength. Jenny felt comfortable around him. He was gorgeous, to put it mildly. And he just so happened to be one of the few men who were taller than she was, even with her high-heeled sandals on. Jenny cautioned herself not to run too far ahead in their friendship. She realized that she had virtually no experience with relationships, and Thomas was a bit older than she.

~Chapter Twenty-two~

"**Thomas, this was here all along.** I missed something that I was yearning for all my life, and it was right in front of my nose!"

Thomas drove up a high ridge and parked his car. Jenny was amazed at the beautiful surroundings. Eighteen years of her life, and Jenny had not ventured more than five miles out of her settlement.

"Are you referring to the terrain, Jenny, or me?" Jenny felt heat rush to her face. She marveled at how much truth was in that question.

"Come, I want to show you something," he said, taking hold of her hand and guiding her up the slope.

No matter what angle Jenny looked, her view was unhindered.

"This must be the highest point on the island," she exclaimed. "Thomas, this is heavenly. How did you find this place?"

Thomas leaned on a huge boulder and explained.

"When my parents died, all I wanted to do was to run, hide, and get lost. I was so young, only nineteen years old."

Jenny climbed on the rock next to Thomas, listening intently to what he had to say.

"I spent lots of time on my dirt bike just driving aimlessly. One day I stumbled upon this place. Several years later, I located the owner and offered to buy it. They weren't interested in selling...until now."

Jenny was overjoyed for Thomas. This was a beautiful piece of property, and soon it would be his.

"Oh Thomas, I don't know anyone else who would be more deserving than you to have this property. I wish you the greatest success with it."

Thomas reached into his pocket and pulled out a little black velvet pouch.

"Jenny," he sat beside her, carefully choosing his words as he rubbed the pouch with his thumb. "I decided last night to close the deal on this property. I always envisaged this property as a haven for me and my family."

He took a white gold and diamond ring from the pouch and held Jenny's hand. "This ring belonged to my mother. I would be honored if you would wear it." Thomas smiled bravely, not entirely sure of what her reaction would be. Jenny was startled.

"Thomas, what are you saying?"

Thomas was determined not to have Jenny walk out of his life again. "Jenny, I want you to be my wife. Please say you will."

Jenny was stunned, virtually speechless. This was like a typical movie scene, but she was no actress, and this was real life.

"I feel like I'm caught up in a whirlwind right now, Thomas. This is all happening too fast for me."

Jenny got up and walked away. She knew that she wasn't thinking clearly. If she were, she would have shouted a resounding, "no!" But she couldn't get it out of her mouth. Every fiber in her being said "yes." Thomas approached her and placed the ring on her finger very slowly, never taking his eyes off hers.

"Jenny, I love you, and if you'll have me, I want us to spend the rest of our lives together."

"Oh my goodness, I wasn't expecting this, Thomas."

Jenny's heart melted. She knew that she had strong feelings for Thomas. She came to that conclusion earlier that morning. She enjoyed his company, he was always decent and respectful to her, but she wasn't sure she knew what love was, but she was sure it was something she should have in her marriage.

"Thomas, I know that I have strong feelings for you—I guess I did love you and Ms. Chloé, but I can't honestly say that I'm in love with you. I'm not sure what that really is."

Thomas lifted Jenny's chin and looked her square in the eyes.

"Can you say that you're not?"

The answer to that could have been easily read through Jenny's eyes. She closed them, hoping to conceal the truth of what was rushing through her heart.

"Answer me, Jenny. I won't give up that easily."

Thomas kissed her hand and pulled her gently to himself. His closeness sending shudders through her body.

"No, Thomas, I can't say that I don't love you. It's just, how do I know that it's not just my hormones getting the best of me?" Thomas laughed. He had never heard anyone put it quite like that before.

"When I'm close to you like this, my knees feel weak, and I don't know what to do. I'm not sure I'm thinking straight. I must sound really silly right now."

He knew that Jenny wanted to be with him, but she resisted him nevertheless. He knew years before but refused to do something about it. They were destined to be together.

"I think you and I both know that we belong together, Jenny. Are you not telling me something? I wish you would tell me exactly

90

what's on your mind. I know you aren't married but are you seeing someone else?"

A cloud swept in front of the sun with a gentle breeze causing Jenny to shiver. Now was as good a time as any to talk about her attempt at a relationship.

"I suppose I should tell you what's on my mind. You've been upfront with me all along." Jenny looked around for a comfortable spot to sit. "Come," she motioned to him, "we can sit over here for a moment if you like, and I'll tell you exactly what my reluctance is all about."

Not knowing what to expect, Thomas prepared himself for the worse. He had everything money could buy. He was a great success in the business arena, but the one thing he wanted most seemed out of his grasp and had been since she left the island.

"Thomas, you are wonderful. I can't imagine anyone not wanting to be your wife—which makes my hesitation even more ridiculous." She turned to him, hoping to make him understand. "I just don't want to mess up or make a hasty decision."

Jenny told Thomas about the only young man she had ever allowed herself to get close to—Jimmy Smith. The people closest to her saw the signs and advised her against the relationship, but she was unyielding, plunging into the relationship.

"It was disastrous, Thomas. I almost married a rapist and a murderer!"

"I'm glad you didn't, Jen. I also believe you know me well enough, Jenny, to know that I do not fit into any of those categories. I'm sorry you went through that ordeal. It's so unfortunate that those kinds of people exist, but please don't make me pay for his mistake."

Thomas understood more than what Jenny had said. More than anything now, he wanted to protect her and care for her. He sensed Jenny had never been intimate with a man before and was somewhat fearful of becoming involved.

"You've experienced many hurts, Jen, but those times are in the past. I want so much to make you happy."

The word "no" didn't seem to be in Thomas' dictionary. Jenny had exhausted every conceivable reason she could think of. She almost convinced herself that their union was not possible. Jenny knew what her real problem was. She had gotten so used to being poorly treated; she didn't know how to handle herself when someone really appreciated her.

"Okay, Thomas, I accept your proposal," she whispered, still not believing that the words actually left her mouth.

Thomas stood up, gave a shout, and embraced her. He wanted to hold her and swing her around but was sure they would both tumble down the hillside if he tried to. He felt as though he had been holding his breath, and now he could finally breathe.

"You have just made me the happiest man in the world, Ms. Jennifer Hanna, and I'll always love you for it."

Jenny held on to Thomas tightly. She felt secure in his arms, and she believed him.

"You won't regret one day of our lives together, Jenny, I promise you. From this day forward, I will soak you shamelessly with every bit of my love."

Tears of joy rolled down Jenny's cheeks. She never dreamed anyone could ever love her, but now that he had said it, she was going to hold him to his promise. In return, she would be the best wife he could possibly dream of. When she finally looked up, trying to compose herself, Jenny realized that Thomas was also crying.

He kissed her gently on her lips—something she had not even permitted Jimmy to do. Jenny thought that her entire body would melt. She smiled bashfully at him. It was even better than she had imagined. Now she didn't want him to stop.

"Thomas, you just caused my toes to curl," Jenny whispered with her eyes still closed, attempting to savor every moment.

Thomas felt exactly what Jenny had tried to put into words.

"We'd better be going now, Jenny, before I find someone to marry us tonight." The way Jenny was feeling, that might not have been a bad idea.

By the time Thomas had taken Jenny to see the resort, it was late. He gave her a brief tour and took her to a quaint restaurant where they enjoyed a light dinner. The resort was even nicer than Thomas had described. He managed to capture the essence of island living, complete with Jenny's favorite native plants. Jenny expected to see coconut trees but to see the imaginative use of the local banana plants, coco plum trees, and even aloe vera arranged with the hibiscus and croton plants was quite amazing.

Rather than having a single structure, the living quarters were duplex-style villas on the beach, each with its own private deck that led to the beach.

"Thomas, this place is absolutely delightful. It's all that you said that you would do and then some."

Thomas nodded appreciatively, "the next time you visit, it must be in full daylight, Jen. Perhaps you can stay for a few days."

Jenny smiled. It was a nice thought. She was amazed at how Thomas' vision for his property had unraveled so beautifully.

~Chapter Twenty-three~

The date was all set. Jenny and Thomas were to be married in April. They both thought the modeling opportunity was one she should look into. It was only scheduled to last ten days if everything went according to schedule. Thomas thought it was a good idea to tour Europe for their honeymoon. He remembered Jenny always longed to travel to the Continent. Afterward, Jenny would try her hand at modeling in Madrid. From there, it was back to their little island hideaway.

Ike knew that his aunt was in love, even if she hadn't realized it herself.

"I hope that means you'll be moving back here," he probed.

"I do believe that you can say that, Ike. Only now, I'm beginning to feel nervous." Ike closed the front door and sat down at the table.

"Aunt Jen, I've only been here for a short time, and during that time, I can say that I have only heard good things about Mr. Ford. He's a decent man. I think marrying him would be a great thing. I really wish you all the best."

\#

By the time Jenny returned to the mainland, word had already spread. Jenny Hanna, from Hiram's Variety, planned to tie the knot with Thomas Ford of Maruba. Jenny was amazed at the number of people that knew and loved Thomas. He was only the island's most eligible bachelor. Gertie screamed when Jenny finally came home. She too had heard the news.

"Girl, you were gone for just about one week and come back almost married! I think I need to take a short vacation too and see what I come up with," she teased her friend.

"Well, you'll have your opportunity, Gert. The wedding will be back home in several months. I would be so honored if you would stand with me. Please say, you will?"

Gertie smiled and nodded as she clasped her friend's hands. She couldn't think of a better person to stand with. The treat, she thought, was hers.

Even Mr. Beneby had grand things to say about Thomas. "I'll be sorry to see you go, Jenny, thas for sure, but y' gat y' self a good man."

Mr. Beneby had taken to the hard-working young lady who had turned his store around and knew she deserved to have someone who genuinely cared for her.

"I wish you all the best. You are one decent girl—you go and have a good life."

Thomas called Jenny every day for the next three weeks.

"Jenny, is there any reason why we're torturing ourselves by being apart?"

Jenny couldn't think of a good reason. She had already gotten Mr. Beneby's blessing and tendered her resignation. She had also informed Gertie that she would pay her share of the rent for the next few months even though she would not be living there.

"Come home, Jenny. I need you here with me."

Jenny hesitated. She wanted to pinch herself. How a simple girl like her could land a wonderful attentive man like Thomas was astounding. What's more, she never had to pursue him.

"Jenny, let's get married this weekend!" Thomas urged. "Ike can be my best man, and Gertie can be your maid of honor."

That was the best idea Jenny heard in days. The longer she stayed away from Thomas, the more she realized how much she really did love him.

"I think it's a great idea, Thomas, except that I don't have a wedding dress yet."

As far as Thomas was concerned, anything Jenny wore would be fine. He just knew that he wasn't willing to have her away from him any longer.

"So it's settled then, Sweetheart? I'll send the airplane to collect you both on Friday. If you haven't found anything there you'd like to wear, you'll find something in one of our boutiques at the resort."

Thomas did better than sending the airplane for Jenny. Much to her surprise, he was the first to step off of the plane to meet her. Jenny ran to him, not at all concerned with the group of bystanders glaring at them. Thomas picked her up and swung her around before he kissed her.

"Thomas, I know now, and it's so wonderful!" she said excitedly, forgetting that she had not formally introduced Gertie to Thomas.

"What is it, Jenny? What is this wonderful news?"

Jenny placed her arms around Thomas' neck and kissed him. "I know, Thomas Ford, beyond a shadow of a doubt that I love you, and you are the only man for me."

Thomas held her close and whispered in her ear. "I could have told you that a long time ago, darling, if you would only listen to me." They both laughed, leaving their spectators guessing as to what the joke was all about.

Thomas signaled to his pilot to ensure that the luggage was loaded on the aircraft. Jenny then introduced Thomas to her friend and roommate, Gertie Taylor.

"Gertie, we finally meet. Thanks for coming down on such short notice. You are truly a good friend." Gertie shook Thomas' hand.

"It's my pleasure. Besides, I just had to see this superman Jenny has been talking about for the past couple of weeks."

Thomas excused himself from the ladies to ensure that the airplane was being refueled and adequately stocked.

"It's a shame Thomas don't have no brothers, Jen. He is some catch!" Gertie leaned over to her friend and pinched her. "Girl, you should have never left the island the first time. Suppose he had gotten away?"

"It is simply destiny, Gert– the right man, the right timing, and of course, the right place."

"Seems to me that you were out lookin' for your gold field in strange pastures and was too blind to see it was in your own back yard."

"Yup," Jenny conceded, "and I almost got caught up with fool's gold."

The two girls laughed as they walked toward the plane. Jimmy certainly wouldn't have taken too kindly to being called fool's gold, but the truth could sometimes hurt. Anyway, Jenny knew that the timing for her and Thomas was just perfect now. She was independent, confident, and knew what she wanted in life.

~Chapter Twenty-four~

Thomas arranged for Jenny, Gertie, and Ike to have personal suites at the resort. Gertie's eyes popped the moment the plane landed at the resort's private airstrip. The property was immaculate, and the service from Thomas' staff was impeccable. After taking them to their suites, Thomas arranged to meet them in the restaurant after they had a chance to clean up and rest.

Rest was the furthest thing from Gertie's mind when she stepped into her suite. The hotel was magnificent. It topped all great Mediterranean resorts she had seen on the "rich and famous" type magazines. Gertie couldn't believe Thomas owned all of this and was still so down to earth. She climbed up on the four-poster bed and lay sprawled across it, moving her hands like a fluttering butterfly.

"Oh lawdy, I must be in heaven," she whispered.

Gertie's room had immaculate dark hardwood flooring, the walls were a soft butternut color, and the sheer off-white drapes at the French doors which led out to her private Jacuzzi blew softly in the wind. Her high four-poster bed with a gazillion pillows on it seemed to be more of a gigantic pillow than a mattress. She just had to test out her cloud bed, as she called it, before she went to dinner. Although the room was already cool, there were two large ceiling fans with dark wicker blades, which helped give the room an upscaled island feel. Each piece of art on the walls had an exquisite wood frame that looked as though it had been dipped in 14-carat gold then aged with a brown patina. The private desk near the oversized sofa was a great place to sit and write letters to family and friends. If she had time, Gertie decided she would do just that.

The bathroom itself was almost as large as and certainly better equipped than the health spa she had decided to join the month before. Gertie unpacked her bags and made her way to the massive bathtub for a relaxing bath. Half an hour later, Gertie was exploring the rest of the suite. The wet bar was stocked with snacks galore, not to mention the fresh juices and soft drinks that lined the racks. It seemed like only minutes had passed when there was a soft knock at the door. Jenny had come to accompany her to the restaurant where they would meet Thomas and Ike.

"Jenny, this place...this place is paradise, Girl," she told her friend pulling her into the room to give her a brief tour.

"It is quite lovely, isn't it," Jenny agreed with her friend, whose eyes were still wide with excitement. "Anyway, we can't keep Thomas waiting—let's make our way over to the great house."

Gertie took one last look at her room and closed the door behind them.

Ike sat fidgeting at the table. He felt self-conscious sitting in a restaurant filled with extremely wealthy people, some of whom he recognized from the television. Thomas did his best to make Ike comfortable, but Ike was too engrossed in everything around them. Occasionally he would marvel at the high ceiling and the intricate woodwork on the door frames. It was evident that Thomas was a man who gave a lot of attention to detail.

All eyes were on Jenny as she and Gertie entered the room. She had on a soft flowing blue and green chiffon dress that gathered at the waist. The neckline and waist were beaded with sparkling gems that made Jenny look as though she was royalty. Jenny was glad she listened to Gertie's suggestion to purchase it for the trip. She especially loved the Roman-style bracelet wrapped around her arm, adding a special touch to her ensemble. Thomas stood and greeted them as they walked towards the table. He kissed Jenny lightly on the cheek and escorted both ladies to their table. Ike and Gertie were so involved in their surroundings that they hardly spoke a word the whole evening.

They barely noticed when Thomas led Jenny to the dance floor, both swaying gently to the soft music barely lifting their feet from the floor. He held his fiancé close, grateful that she had agreed to come to him earlier than planned. The jazz band played old favorites through the night, totally oblivious that the guests had begun to trickle out, leaving only their table occupied.

"Excuse me, Sir." Ike had tapped Thomas on his shoulder and bowed graciously to his aunt. "May I have the honor?"

"You're too much, Ike."

"Aunt Jen, I just want you to know that I feel honored to be a part of your wedding. I wish you great success in your marriage. Mr. Ford, I mean Uncle Thomas is a great guy, and you deserve each other."

Jenny was touched. She held her nephew for a moment and kissed his cheek.

"Thank you, Ike. That meant a whole lot to me. But the honor is mine, having my handsome nephew stand in my wedding."

The band finished their last tune. It was late, and though she was extremely excited and believed that sleep was the furthest thing from her mind, Jenny thought it best to get as much rest as she could that evening. After all, she had to look absolutely stunning tomorrow. Ike escorted Gertie to her suite and then ventured to his, while Thomas accompanied Jenny to her suite. It had been a full, exciting day. By eleven o'clock the following morning, Jenny would be Mrs. Jennifer Ford.

~Chapter Twenty-five~

"**I**t's such a beautiful day..." Jenny leaned against her open French door breathing in the fresh morning air.

It was delightful being so near to the ocean again. She took a sip of her hot tea while savoring the sights. The gulls were chirping away as they flew past her on the way to the marina. A few boats were already slipping harbor for their early fishing trips. Room service delivered her breakfast of scrambled eggs and grits, but she was just too excited to eat all of it, so she thought she would make do with the tea and an apple.

"I didn't know I could be this happy," Jenny whispered to herself.

The alarm clock went off for her wake-up call. Jenny smiled—there was no way she could oversleep on her special day. She wanted to call Thomas, but Gertie made them promise not to communicate anymore before the ceremony.

Gertie would be over in less than half an hour to help her with her hair and makeup. Her friend was the closest thing to a sister she had ever known.

\#

Jenny felt as though she was in a dream as she made her way gracefully towards the white gazebo, which stood ablaze with deep pink bougainvillea vines intricately wrapped around its posts as it scaled to the top of the roof. The scene was idyllic. The ocean breeze mingled with fresh-cut grass and aromatic fragrances from the flowers that draped the pathway was heavenly. The weather had cooperated beyond Jenny's expectations. Though she walked as if there were a myriad of guests ensconced about them, Jenny and Thomas had the entire lagoon to themselves, except a few curious onlookers.

Thomas' heart beat wildly as he gazed at Jenny walking towards him. His light tan suit with an open-collared white shirt with gold cuff links was typical of Thomas' dress-down elegant style. A single violinist played softly in the background as Ike escorted his aunt to her waiting groom before taking his place as the best man. Gertie had insisted on Jenny selecting the wispy white, calf-length gown whose neckline was sprinkled with pearls, seed beads, and meticulously stitched rhinestones that glimmered in the light. Her pear-shaped pearl-like earrings were the only jewelry she wore except for the ring Thomas had previously given her. Jenny's attire right down to the mid-heel ivory pumps was simply elegant. Once again, Gertie had done a winning job on Jenny. Her hair was superb, and her face radiant.

"Jen, you're breathtaking," Thomas whispered into her ear. Jenny smiled modestly. As she was about to tell him how dashing he looked, the old preacher cleared his throat to inform them that the service was underway.

"Let me get all my business out of the way, son, then you can talk to her all you want," he said, grinning mischievously.

Jenny didn't know who the gentleman was, but she was grateful that he could come on such short notice.

"Love is more than a feeling, young people. Right now, you feel all bubbly inside, but that ain't how it's always gonna be," he cautioned them. "There are going to be days when this love you feel is tested. But," he paused, looking at them sternly, his gray hair seeming to authenticate his wisdom despite his wearied appearance. "You have to understand that to make this marriage

102

work, it will take commitment, patience, and a decision to love in spite of what you see and feel at times. Storms will come in your life, but you can't get stuck in them, no, you gatta keep movin', you gatta go through to the other side. Trust God, and you'll make it."

The old preacher's words of encouragement touched Jenny's heart. She didn't have much exposure to church and what people called the Christian life as she was growing up on the island, though there seemed to be an unspoken code of decency that resonated through many of the older folks. It just happened to skip her house.

At the close of the ceremony, the old man joined the couple's hands together and patted them gently.

"Young people, it ain't money that will make your marriage work, neither sex although," he said smiling, "all two of 'em will help to make it a lot easier. I want to encourage you two to put God first in your relationship. If you don't know him, then you should get to know him 'cause he is someone you can turn to in every situation."

He turned around, picked up his Bible from the bench, and passed it to Thomas, smiling. "Son, this is the best gift you could ever be given. The key to life is within these pages."

With that, the old man gave the couple his blessings and, with a subtle air of mischief, told them that they were free to be one. The service was short and sweet but meaningful. Gertie sniffled throughout the ceremony. Jenny and Thomas were so beautiful together, and he treated her friend with such care. Gertie cried all the more, knowing that she would not see Jenny for a good while.

Ike stood quietly, taking in everything that was happening around him. He had never seen a couple so wrapped up in each other before. He wondered if his parents had ever been in love before. Ike shrugged his shoulders and stuffed his hands in his pockets. He doubted it. If his father ever showed any outright affection to his mother, it was probably a long, long time ago. His mother was not an easy person to live with—not that his dad was some jewel himself. Jenny and Thomas had given him a sense of hope for relationships. Perhaps two people could care for each other and act sensibly towards each other if they put their mind to it.

Thomas took his new bride by the hand and pulled her close to him before turning to the old man.

"Reverend Sammy, thank you, you have just made me the happiest man on the face of this earth."

"Well, son, you may now kiss your bride."

"With pleasure."

Gertie and Ike joined in as the onlookers cheered as Thomas kissed his wife gently on her lips.

~Chapter Twenty-six~

Acool soft gust of wind blew through the French doors of the honeymoon suite, sending soft billows of the sheer drapery floating in the air. It had been such a glorious evening that Thomas left the patio doors to their upstairs bedroom open as they reveled in the fresh air. The night still fresh in his mind, Thomas reached out to embrace his wife once more.

He enjoyed looking at her as much as he did making love to her. At first, Jenny was nervous. She constantly covered herself with the sheet, not wanting him to look at her nakedness. The moon lent a soft light to the room, taking the edge off Jenny's concern for the lamps being left on. Thomas was not modest in the least. He wanted his eyes to drink in every bit of his beautiful wife. He dreamed of this day for so long he would not let even a sheet come between the two of them.

When Jenny had finally awakened to the gentle lapping of the waves against the sandy beach, she lay in bed gazing at her husband, completely absorbed in the memories of their first evening as husband and wife. It was ten o'clock, and Jenny had gotten up to refresh herself and indulge in the morning's fresh-baked bread with a glass of mango juice. Thomas rolled over, opening his eyes, scanning the room for his wife once again.

"Here you are, Sweetheart." She remembered that he loved fresh fruits for breakfast and set them on the nightstand next to the bed. After breakfast and a quick trip to the bathroom, they both made their way back to their bed.

Several hours later, Jenny turned to look at the clock again. It was lunchtime. Thomas held onto his wife and kissed her forehead before easing from the bed.

"If I didn't know any better, Jenny, I would have guessed that I could live strictly off of your love."

Jenny giggled and pulled her husband towards her. She was so happy being close to him.

The elaborate dinner setting still graced the suite as neither Thomas nor Jenny had eaten the entire night. She wasn't sure if it was hunger or nervousness she was experiencing when Thomas carried her into their suite. However, sensing her modesty, Thomas was the epitome of warmth. His tenderness towards her quickly lessened her uneasiness, and with it, silencing all thought of food.

"Hon, I had a few plans on standby for us today, but I'll leave it to your fancy. If you like," he added mischievously, "we can lock ourselves in for the entire day, or we can have a wonderful day on the ocean. I have our yacht on standby, and lunch is being prepared for a day out."

Jenny wrapped the sheet around herself and sat on Thomas' lap as he took another bite of the fresh melon.

"Whatever you want to do is fine with me, Darling. As long as we spend this day together, it doesn't really matter what we do."

Thomas placed a small piece of melon in Jenny's mouth and kissed her gently. Being intimate with Thomas came so naturally.

"I think we had better go out, Jen, lest I forget that we have our whole lives together, and I attempt to make love to you all day."

Jenny laughed, "You're impossible, Thomas!" She quickly stood up and walked towards the bathroom, quite aware of her husband's eyes lingering on her.

"Dress cool and casual," he called after her. "We have a full day ahead."

#

The day couldn't have been better if she had planned it herself. Although the sun was out, there was a soft cool breeze in the air. Sleek yachts lined the marina, reeking unashamedly of wealth. Jenny stopped short in her tracks as Thomas led her to his boat. She stood on the dock, her hands akimbo and mouth agape. Thomas shrugged his shoulders and smiled at her reaction. Her name stood emblazoned on the modest eighty-foot cabin cruiser that was moored to the jetty.

"It's been on there for several years," he boasted, "you have been etched on my heart for some time."

"Oh Thomas, I was so blind it was pathetic." Jenny stared at her name, shaking her head in bewilderment.

"I'm the happiest man on earth right now, Jen. I don't even want to think about those empty years without you. C'mon," Thomas extended his hand to Jenny, guiding her over the gangway—"we have several hours of light left. Let's be on our way."

Jenny looked around, there was no one else to be seen aboard the yacht.

"Who's going to drive this thing?" she asked excitedly.

"I was considering letting you have a go at it, Jen, but that might just delay our return today as planned," Thomas teased. "Actually, the crew is below deck making ready for our departure."

A few minutes later, an older gentleman emerged from below. "How do you do today, Ma'am," he asked politely. "Sir," he turned to Thomas, "we can cast off at your pleasure."

Thomas shook the gentleman's hand briskly.

"Good, Captain Isaac, we are ready now. Oh, Captain Isaac," he smiled brightly, turning to his new bride, "this is my lovely wife, Mrs. Jennifer Ford, the young lady you have been hearing about for some time."

Isaac grinned coyly at Jenny, "It's a pleasure, Ma'am, and congratulations to you both."

"Thank you, Captain Isaac. It's a pleasure to meet you."

Jenny continued to look around the vessel as Thomas and Captain Isaac made ready to leave the dock. She wanted to pinch herself. Could someone like her really be experiencing such happiness? Jenny quietly hoped it would never come to an end.

~Chapter Twenty-seven~

"This past week has been** wonderful, Thomas, hasn't it?" Thomas nodded in agreement as he stared into the horizon. "Thomas, I understand that you must return to your work tomorrow. It would be selfish of me not to let you go."

He took her slender hand and tapped it lightly.

"I've had this business trip planned for some months now, Jen. It's very important, and I was unsuccessful in rescheduling it."

Jenny leaned on the patio, railing next to her husband. They had their entire life before them; she couldn't begrudge him a little business trip.

"Where will you be off to, and when will you return?"

Thomas guided Jenny to the cozy wooden swing where they had spent the last several evenings watching the sunset.

"I'll be in London for a few days, and then Zurich to meet with my bankers," he paused briefly, "I would have loved to have taken you with me, sweetheart, but I'm afraid the meetings are quite lengthy, and we wouldn't have much time to spend together," he explained.

Jenny was not perturbed. She knew how to use her time wisely. Though she would miss Thomas, she thought it an excellent opportunity to embrace the project they had spoken of days before.

"Thomas, I'll get started on the children's library in the village. That should occupy my time."

Thomas was relieved. The week away would quickly pass, and in no time, they would have gone on their official honeymoon.

"I've opened two bank accounts in both of our names, Jen—one is for the general running of the house, and the other is for your pleasure. I'll be gone only a short time, but I will call every day."

Jenny thought she would stay with Ike in the village until Thomas returned. She would be closer to the old building she wanted Ike to convert for her and would be happy for his company. Thomas had an even better idea.

"Honey, if you don't mind, why don't you have Ike move into the house with you while I'm gone? I'd feel much better knowing that I could contact you there by telephone."

It was a good idea, Jenny agreed. She thought it wise to begin settling in their home as soon as possible. Living in the hotel was terrific, but without Thomas to share it with her, she would much rather return to the north. Jenny accompanied Thomas to his private aircraft the following day. He planned on flying to the mainland, where he would board a connecting flight to London. Shortly after, Jenny drove home to share her idea with Ike.

Ike was thrilled with both ideas. The thought of transforming the old vacant building in the village was a fantastic idea. It would take a few dollars to overhaul it, but he was up for the challenge. He did not relish the thought of his aunt being on the hill by herself while Thomas was away either, even though most of the villagers still slept with their doors and windows open on the island.

Although there was a telephone in Thomas' house, not many people had telephones of their own. To make phone calls, they had to visit the local government office where an operator was stationed. The village was improving, nonetheless. Since Jenny left several years ago, most homes had now been updated with electricity and indoor plumbing. Progress was being made on the tiny island, and Jenny wanted the village's children to be prepared for it.

Jenny's childhood teacher, Ms. Trotman, had come and gone from the little schoolhouse, but she had left an indelible mark on Jenny in the process. Jenny wanted to create the same hunger for information and education in the youngsters in her village and the surrounding villages. Thomas was honored when Jenny thought to name the center after his grandmother.

In no time, Ike was knee-deep in work. He and Jenny spent long hours restoring the old building. By the third day, the activity had drawn so much attention from the young men in the village that they dropped by after their chores to help with the project. Jenny hadn't realized that there was such a hunger in the young men for activity. Now that they had been allowed to make a positive contribution to their village, less dominoes were being smacked against the makeshift table beneath the large shady tree.

With the team of youngsters working tirelessly on the inside and another group outside, the building was finished two days before Thomas' arrival. Ike had already begun building study tables and benches for the homework area and had delegated the task of constructing library shelves to two other youngsters. Another area was made ready for the three new computers and desks, which were due in, along with a selection of books, in another week or so.

Several persons in the village began collecting used books and leaving them on Jenny's doorstep. As word spread through the community, messages were sent for Jenny to collect used schoolbooks, encyclopedias, dictionaries, and a heap of novels. Blake Smith made his taxi available to collect the books from anyone who had anything readable.

The project was becoming a community effort as residents began taking pride in the Chloé Ford Center. Both Jenny and Thomas had planned to pay for the entire project themselves, but with the effort of their neighbors, the joint endeavor began to take on new meaning.

It was only the yard needing to be cleaned and grassed and the electrician to complete his work—then the center would be ready for the second phase. Jenny thanked all of her helpers immensely and showed her gratitude by treating them and their families to a barbeque by the village square.

Never had the town remembered such unity and selflessness. Many could hardly believe it was their Jenny who was behind the latest goings-on in the town. Jenny Hanna had never warranted a second glance. Now she was back and pouring into her community the love she had yearned for as a child.

With all the work virtually completed on the center, Thomas and Jenny embarked upon their long-awaited honeymoon to Europe. Ike promised to supervise the remaining tasks and look into various persons to assist with the running of the center. Traveling had been one of Jenny's ambitions from her earliest days on the island—she had looked forward to visiting France in particular, having read so much about the Eiffel tower.

~Chapter Twenty-eight~

From planes to trains and boats to underground transportation, Jenny had almost done it all. The few days spent on the Swiss Alps were beyond Jenny's wildest imaginations. The air in the mountains was crisp and cool, refreshing but quite different from the sweet ocean breeze on which she had grown up. Italy was probably her favorite stop, as they toured wonderful sites such as the leaning tower of Pisa and took romantic gondola rides through the quaint city of Venice.

Because of the varied climates, Jenny spent quite a sum of money on clothing she was sure she might not need regularly. The stores themselves were magnificent. They had the finest couture imaginable, not that Jenny knew that much about fashion. Thomas had to insist on Jenny indulging. He had seen her eyes pop when glancing at the price tags on a few occasions. Several weeks in Europe did not change the fact that Jenny was still an island girl.

Jenny knew Gertie would have loved to spend a day just window-shopping in some of the exclusive boutiques that lined the streets. She knew her friend would be thrilled with the outfit she purchased for her.

Thomas spent much of his youth in Europe in boarding schools and on little jaunts with his friends on mid-term breaks. With Jenny, however, he felt like he was seeing it again for the first time.

113

Somehow, he took the natural beauty for granted but saw it from a refreshed perspective as he traveled with Jenny.

Jenny realized that the books she read over the years were great in exposing her to the new cultures, but they did little to prepare her for the aura or charm of the big cities and the quaint cobbled streets sprinkled throughout the towns. A part of their experience was frequenting a host of eateries whose allure and aroma beckoned them to taste their exciting wares. Jenny sampled just about everything from fine restaurants, corner kiosks, and colorful roadside merchants peddling their colorful native flowers, pastries, and local delicacies.

By the time Jenny and Thomas had settled into their hotel suite in Spain, Jenny felt somewhat wearied.

"Perhaps I've eaten a little too much today, Thomas. I'm going to have an early night if you don't mind."

After an entire month of traveling through Europe and tasting virtually every delicacy there was, Jenny was feeling unsettled.

"You get your rest, Sweetheart. Tomorrow is your big day in front of the camera," Thomas reminded her. "I have these journals to keep my company for a while."

Their fast-paced honeymoon had culminated in Madrid, Spain, just as they planned. Eric had called earlier that day to confirm the time and place for their meeting the following day. Thomas wondered if all the excitement at the bullfight had added to his wife's nervous stomach. He made a pot of herbal tea for his wife and set it on the table near their bed.

Neither of them realized how tired they both were. By eight o'clock, they were fast asleep. Jenny lay gracefully over their bed while Thomas slept still fully clothed with a book across his chest.

The city was awake well before dawn as Jenny breathed in the freshly brewed coffee and breakfast muffins. As great and tempting as the aroma was, Jenny dared not venture into any food before her meeting. Thomas had already risen and was almost dressed by the time Jenny climbed from their bed. She sneaked quietly behind him and embraced him as he reached into the closet for a shirt.

"Had a good night?" Jenny asked, squeezing her husband tightly. Thomas turned and held her long.

"It was quite nice. How was your rest?" he asked, tipping Jenny's chin upwards to look into her eyes.

"Marvelous, Darling, and I'm ready to conquer the world!"

"I believe you are," Thomas agreed, turning her towards the bathroom. "But after you've changed from your night clothes."

Jenny laughed as she hurried into the shower. Their drive would take about an hour if they were to beat the traffic.

"I'll be out in a jiffy, don't you worry. That tea was great last night, Hon. I'd love to have another cup if you wouldn't mind putting some more on."

Thomas glanced at the morning news while he put on a fresh pot of tea.

The drive was subdued, except for the music that tinkered through the radio of their rental car. Jenny was engrossed in the fashion magazines she purchased at the corner kiosk the day before. She had no experience in modeling and was hoping to get some tips from the ladies that graced the pages. Thomas knew that she would be a natural and told her as much. He was more concerned about the hours she would be required to work, as the shoot had been crammed into three days due to Eric's inescapable meeting in South Africa.

Nonetheless, Eric was thrilled to see his friends again. He stood waiting at the top of the stairs as they pulled in front of the site. A whole team of people had already busied themselves with lighting, fans, and other pieces of props and scenery. Jenny squeezed Thomas' hand as they walked up the steps.

"Am I doing the right thing, Darling?" she asked. "I don't want to make an absolute fool of myself."

Before Thomas could answer her, Eric was at their side. He waved to a young lady who came dashing down the steps towards them.

"Jenny, I am thrilled you made it. And even happier you got the most eligible bachelor off the market." Eric smiled at his friend while shaking his hand. "Now, I must tend to all the broken hearts that never got the opportunity to steal him away."

Thomas laughed. "You are quite dangerous, my friend."

"Jenny, Darling, this is Melanie. She will assist you with your wardrobe. Whatever you need, Melanie is here for you." Melanie grinned at Jenny as she shook her hand.

"I saw the photos Eric took of you. You are even more exotic in person." Jenny turned and looked at Thomas who shrugged an "I told you so" look.

"Thank you, Melanie. I appreciate all the help you can give me."

Jenny thought Melanie would make a wonderful model herself. She had a full head of long strawberry curls and beautiful green eyes with enormous eyelashes. Melanie was slender and had a personality as vibrant as her hair.

"We're going to be shooting evening wear today, Mrs. Ford, so after I've gotten you measured up, I'll take you over to Jaz, our stylist, who will work on your hair and make-up."

It was almost eleven-thirty when Jenny finally emerged from her transformation. She could hardly believe her eyes when she looked in the mirror. The clothes were from one of the great fashion houses in Paris. As soon as she took note of her hair, Jenny laughed uncontrollably. She had come all the way from a little island in the West Indies to have a great fashion stylist twist her hair in what would be considered an everyday style back home. Despite the laughter, Jenny had to admit, the look was so stunning she barely recognized herself.

"Aha, I knew it!" shouted Eric as he spotted Jenny walking towards him. "Just be natural, Jenny," he said, snapping his camera before she even reached the set.

"Chin up, that's it. All right, you stand still. Keep looking over there. I'll do all the moving." Eric moved as stealthily as a cat as he climbed high and lunged low to capture the perfect shot.

By the end of the shoot, Jenny had changed into six of the most fabulous gowns she had ever laid eyes on. Thomas waited behind the scenes for Jenny, not wanting to distract her from the beautiful job he thought she was doing. They had a brief lunch together before resuming her schedule, and now he could see fatigue dripping off of her.

"Excellent day! Simply marvelous, Jenny," exclaimed Eric. "You'd better get some rest now, soak your feet and eat a good meal. Tomorrow is an even bigger day."

Melanie guided Jenny to her changing room. "You did great today. I can see that you'll be busy for quite some time. Quite frankly, Mrs. Ford, you're just the boost that the fashion industry needed."

Jenny struggled into her own modest clothing and thanked Melanie and Jaz before skirting off to Thomas who was patiently waiting for her.

~Chapter Twenty-nine~

"**T**his is all so exhilarating!**"** Jenny thought as she moved confidently to Eric's directives. Giving an impromptu twirl before moving to her next change of clothing, she flung her long slender arms in the air towards Melanie and shouted, "I love this work!"

Eric gave Melanie a thumbs up for the next scene. He was counting on Jenny's enthusiasm and Melanie's persuasiveness to move Jenny into the swimsuit collection without much ado. He knew that she had indicated her desire not to take part in this collection but was sure that it was just a case of anxiety.

Much to Eric's chagrin, the ado was meant to be. Jenny stood her ground. As much as she had enjoyed her work so far, she was willing to walk away had Eric insisted on her wearing the scantily made costumes.

"Wild horses cannot drag me into those skimpy swimsuits, Eric," she said, tapping her feet, her hands folded in front of her.

"What about if we made a few minor adjustments, Darling," Eric continued to press.

"Not even with a cape, Eric!"

Jenny signaled to Melanie. "You can get my clothing ready, Melanie. I think we're through for the day."

Eric smiled to himself. Not only did the woman have class, but she was a little fireball. She handled herself like a pro. He had to admit that he respected her all the more for it knowing that it usually took half the amount of time to convince most conservative models to do the same kind of shoot.

"Okay, Jenny," he called to her, "you win, no swimsuits, but since this is your last day with us, grant me a few more hours for more resort wear."

Eric smiled when Jenny's countenance brightened.

"Alright, Eric, but for the record again, I am not prepared to wear scanty items that expose close to or more than underwear. You know we already discussed this."

Eric breathed a sigh of relief. His time was fast eroding.

"Come on, people," he urged his team, "time is money. Let's get this show on the road."

Looking around, he spotted Jaz, who had just gotten comfortable with a soft drink on a nearby chair.

"Today, Jaz, I need your skills today!"

Jaz quickly grabbed her touch-up kit and restored Jenny's make-up seconds before Eric's camera began snapping once more.

#

Jenny washed the last bit of make-up from her face and collapsed onto the chaise next to Thomas. She sat quietly, hoping to repress the wave of nausea that seemed to rise inside. Within seconds Jenny was up and in the bathroom, emptying her lunch in the lavatory. Thomas had noticed a slight change in her demeanor several days before but had summed it up to a nervous stomach.

"I'm calling the doctor, Jen," he cautioned her after helping her back to the chaise.

Despite his efforts to conceal his feelings, Thomas' face brimmed with concern. Unsure of what to do or what to give his wife, Thomas stroked her hair, hoping to soothe her discomfort. Almost an hour later, there was a knock at the door.

"Señor Ford," a white-haired gentleman, with a polite smile barely creasing his face, greeted him. "You called for a doctor. How can I help you?"

Thomas ushered the man in, recognizing his crisp white medical attire with a shiny stethoscope draped around his neck.

"Yes, of course," he said, motioning to his wife, who lay lethargically across the chaise lounge. "I called for assistance for my wife." The old man nodded and smiled at Thomas.

"You leave it to me," he said, his words confidently rolling from his lips. "I'll talk with you after I have examined her." Thomas looked at Jenny, assuring her of his presence.

"Call me, Sweetheart, if you need me."

Jenny nodded as she sat up, rubbing her stomach.

"My dear, I'm Dr. Atala, tell me what you are feeling, and I will do my best to relieve you of this discomfort."

After enlightening Dr. Atala of the sensations she had been experiencing, Jenny further indicated that she felt it was perhaps something she had eaten that had not agreed with her. After examining and questioning his patient, Dr. Atala packed his medical kit and smiled again at Jenny.

"I will give you something to settle your stomach, my dear, but I assure you, you are not sick in the least." He took Jenny's hand and rested it gently on her stomach, "You are going to have a baby."

Thomas could not help but overhear what Dr. Atala had just told his wife. He strode excitedly into the room and sat beside his wife.

"Did you hear, Thomas?" Jenny asked, her face radiant with delight.

"I heard, Darling, and I think it's wonderful news."

Dr. Atala looked at his watch and picked up his belongings. He had one more visit in the hotel before leaving for home. He was hoping that his next call would be as pleasant as this one.

"You will need to get some rest, young lady. The bad feelings will soon pass."

Thomas stood up and shook the doctor's hand. He thanked him profusely for his visit as he escorted him to the door. Thomas seemed to have a million questions race through his mind. The old man, sensing this, put his hand on Thomas' shoulder, reassuring him of his findings.

"When you return home, son, have your family physician do a more thorough check. They will sit with you and answer all of your concerns. For right now, though," he said, reaching for the door, "your wife is fine. She needn't over-exert herself but walks in the fresh air will do wonders for her."

Jenny sat pensively as she waited for Thomas to show the doctor out. She hadn't stopped to think about having children so soon. Everything was happening so quickly for her. It almost felt as if she were caught in a whirlwind.

"Thomas," she said as he walked towards her, "is this alright with you? I know we didn't plan it, and I guess I should have taken the necessary precautions..." Jenny rubbed her stomach, hoping to soothe the wave of nausea she was feeling.

"The most important thing to me right now, Jenny, is your comfort and health. We didn't plan this but believe me, I'm thrilled."

He leaned over and kissed away a tear that trickled down his wife's cheek. Jenny threw her arms around her husband and nestled her head upon his chest.

"Thomas, you know, it's an incredible experience to know that I am actually carrying our baby."

~Chapter Thirty~

Eric called several hours before Thomas and Jenny were scheduled to fly home. He had tried to reach them several times from South Africa, but the circuits were unusually busy.

"Finally," he shouted over the crackling telephone line, "I've been trying to reach you both for days."

Thomas motioned to Jenny to come to the phone, "It's Eric, Hon. He's calling from South Africa." Jenny stood nervously at Thomas' side, waiting for some news on the shoot. "That's fantastic," he shouted to Eric, sticking his finger in his ear.

Jenny was curious, "What's fantastic, Hon?" she whispered, tugging at his arm.

"Here," he shouted over the noisy telephone line, "I'll let you tell her the good news, and then perhaps she can give you our great news!" Jenny grabbed the outstretched phone from her husband.

"Eric, what's the fantastic news?" she begged.

"Oh, it's only that your shoot was a hit and several agencies wish to sign you for the rest of the year. We can chat about it later, and you can decide who you would like to go with. And by the way," he paused, "you made the front cover of Cosmopolitan magazine. I sent one in the mail to you yesterday. It won't hit the newsstands for another month."

"I don't know what to say, Eric. You're brilliant. I couldn't have done it without you."

Eric disagreed. "Well, that quick turnaround isn't the norm, Jenny, but there was an opening, and we were ready to go through. Anyway, don't underestimate yourself, kid. You're a natural, you're gorgeous, and you can be successful at this!"

Using his contacts at the magazine and the fashion houses was an easy feat for Eric. After sitting with execs and showing them the photos from Jenny's shoot, they quickly took the leap of faith with Eric. Jenny was a no-name, and they usually needed more time to plan their cover. Of course, knowing the ins and outs of the industry, Eric had an answer at every turn, assuring them of Jenny's ability to energize the fashion world. He knew that they would not regret it.

Jenny laughed; Eric was lavishing his compliments as usual.

"So what's your good news, Jenny? Don't keep me in suspense..." Before Jenny could answer him, the telephone line gave its last crackle and disconnected.

Thomas stood with tickets in hand, checking his watch. In all of the excitement they had almost forgotten that their limousine driver was waiting to carry them to the airport. Jenny scanned the hotel room, making one last check for any items she might be leaving behind.

"I'm ready," she sang out as she walked over to her husband who stood patiently at the door.

"Good, so am I." The honeymoon was wonderful but they were both eager to return to the island and settle into their own environment.

~Chapter Thirty-one~

Jenny received a welcome that she had never expected. Ike, the young helpers from the center, and the villagers cheered as they drove through the settlement. So proud of his aunt's accomplishments, Ike eagerly told people of Jenny's modeling success. Rising from a state of complete dread with no natural hope of escaping from a mundane lifestyle, Jenny symbolized hope to her people.

Ike embraced his aunt proudly as she sat strapped inside Thomas' sports convertible.

"Aunt Jen, I am so proud of you. Just look at you," he smiled brightly, pulling at her new sporty outfit.

"So, my friend," Jenny whispered to her nephew, "who leaked word to you about my modeling?"

Ike flexed his shoulder, pretending to have a slew of important contacts.

"You know me, Aunt Jen, people just know how to find me." Jen threw her head back laughing at his lame attempt of super importance.

"The truth be told, a reporter called your house while you were away. He wanted to interview you about your new success. Of course, I pretended to know what he was talking about to get more information out of him. Needless to say," he said grinning, "my strategy worked."

Thomas chuckled as he stretched his hand out to Ike for a handshake.

"I see we will need to hire this young man as your public relations manager, Jen."

"We have so much catching up to do, Ike. I want to hear all about our project since we left. If you're available, why don't you join Thomas and me for dinner tomorrow evening?"

Thomas leaned over to Jenny and kissed her softly on her cheek. He looked over to Ike, who was grinning from ear to ear.

"Y'all stop that now," Ike teased them, "before you get yourselves in trouble."

"It's too late for that warning, isn't it, Thomas?" Jenny teased. "That's one of the surprises we wanted to share with you tomorrow."

Ike's mouth dropped open with astonishment.

"You two sure don't waste no time. Anyway," he said, tapping the car and waving them off, "you can fill me in on the details tomorrow. Just know that I will be coming with a very healthy appetite too!"

The months ahead proved exceptionally full for both Thomas and Jenny. It was back to work as usual for her industrious husband and for Jenny. Coping with her general tasks, the center, and now her pregnancy was somewhat of a challenge. Unsure of what she was supposed to be experiencing in her body, Thomas was becoming concerned for his wife and urged her to slow down for the duration of the pregnancy.

"All we have on our hands is time to become involved in various activities, Jen," he cautioned. "My priority is seeing that you and our baby remain strong and healthy."

At the rate Jenny was going, he wondered if she was taking on too many responsibilities. Initially, Jenny grumbled, thinking that busying herself kept her thoughts off of the discomfort she was experiencing. However, for the sake of Thomas' peace of mind, she yielded to her husbands' wishes.

~Chapter Thirty-two~

It was as though history had repeated itself again, this time through Jenny's daughter Cassandra. Cassandra Ford was a fireball of energy. She was quick-witted and knew exactly what she wanted and how she would get it. At ten years of age, Cassie had blossomed into a beauty. Tall and slender like her mother, Cassie's brown skin, shiny black hair, and light brown eyes were captivating. Despite the similarities shared with Jenny, Cassandra Ford was her father's child. Her looks and mannerisms were strictly Thomas'.

"Whatever has gotten into you, Cassandra Ford?" Jenny yelled at her daughter from the front porch, her disheveled little girl plodding up the hill as though nothing had happened.

"Oh nothing, Mama, I just had to settle a score, that's all," Cassie answered her mother matter-of-factly, pushing her bicycle into a nearby hedge of hibiscus plants. Quite like her mother's youthful days, Cassie was the brunt of many an unkind joke in the village; which more often than not, was settled anywhere the ground was flat enough to tussle.

"Well, Cassie, now it's my turn to settle the score. You get yourself in the shower right now. When you're through, young lady, you meet me on the back porch."

The Ford's housekeeper Bloneva stood at the kitchen window eavesdropping on Jenny and Cassie. She smirked to herself. There never seemed to be a day when little Miss Cassie didn't come home with one of her stories. If it wasn't someone calling her names, some little boy was pushing sticks in the spoke of her bicycle when she rode past. Cassie figured if she was going to fall and get dirty, she might as well settle it once and for all with the tormentor.

Rinsing the soap suds from her hands, Bloneva quickly wiped them dry on her apron, making her way to Cassie's room to help clean her up. By the time the child was refreshed and neatly groomed, Bloneva had hoped Ms. Jenny would have forgotten Cassie's encounter in the village. No one in the house was happy when Cassie got spanked, including Jenny. But she figured if talking didn't help her daughter understand, perhaps a gentle reminder of the paddle on her posterior would.

"Sit still, Child," Bloneva tugged at one of the many braids she had set in neat rows across the child's head.

"Ow, that hurts, Ms. Bloneva," she cringed, holding the side of her head.

"Chile, you know that pain is nothin' compared to what you'll feel if your mama remembers what you did today!"

Cassie knew Bloneva had a point. It was better to suffer through a head full of tight plaits and impress her mother than to let her head full of uncontrollable curls dangle across her eyes at a time like this. Jenny loved to see her daughter well-groomed. Cassie felt it had something to do with the temperature. If something were loud, misplaced, or untidy, Jenny would act irritably, as though she was bothered by unrelenting heat.

Whatever it took to soothe the situation, Bloneva was ready to make it happen. She loved little Cassie as though she were her own child. She remembered the day well when the Ford's had returned from their honeymoon. Though Jenny wasn't far along in her pregnancy, Thomas fussed over her like a mother hen protecting her chicks. Within weeks the whole town was alight with the news of Jenny's pregnancy. Several weeks later, Thomas insisted on Jenny hiring Bloneva to help care for her and then look after the child when she was born.

Apart from the first five months of morning sickness, nobody would have guessed that Jenny was even pregnant. Some days were better than others, Bloneva thought, but on those days when Jenny had a particular craving for fried fish or broiled crawfish tails, Bloneva was challenged. Having spent hours preparing and cooking the meals for her boss, Jenny would roll from her favorite spot on the hammock and race to the bathroom at the smell of the food, only to insist that Bloneva get rid of it immediately lest her stomach overturns again. It seemed like forever before Jenny would settle down to eat a meal.

It wasn't until Jenny's seventh month of pregnancy that she began to show physical signs of being with child. Despite her size, Jenny was confident her child was alive and well. Even though she had no medical experience, she figured any baby who could kick as hard and as often as her baby had to be okay. And so she was.

~Chapter Thirty-three~

Bloneva remembered that it was a dismal afternoon when Cassie decided to make her grand entrance to the world. The sky cracked with lightning, brightening the grey blanket of clouds that draped itself around the island. Bloneva had sensed Jenny's discomfort the whole day as she winced and blew at the flood of pain that began to show itself more regularly. A short while after Bloneva had called for the doctor, he was on their doorstep. He would have preferred Jenny's coming to the clinic, but Thomas was not there to transport her.

Not even a half-hour after the doctor had arrived did little Miss Cassie make her stirring entrance. She came out kicking and wailing like a prizefighter. From the moment Bloneva held the darling little fuzzyheaded girl in her arms, they bonded. When Thomas had arrived home several hours later, he raced toward his bedroom, having seen the doctor's car parked in the driveway. Bloneva had heard the familiar sound of his car pull into the yard, as it did every day around the same time.

"Mr. Thomas," she said beaming, hoping to allay the concerned looked that etched his face. "Oh, Mr. Thomas, you've got yourself a beautiful little girl in there, and Ms. Jenny is doing just fine."

Thomas raced to his bedroom to see his wife. Jenny lay propped up among a heap of pillows as she held their baby girl. Jenny smiled at her husband, who radiated at the sight of her and their newborn child.

"You look well, Darling," he whispered before kissing his wife. Jenny propped Cassie up and turned her around for her daddy to see. Thomas stared at his child. She was beautiful. She didn't cry much, but her tiny golden brown legs seemed to peddle at the slightest sound in the room.

"I've finished examining your wife, Mr. Ford," Dr. Taylor said confidently. "Happy to say all is well with her and the baby."

Thomas shook the doctor's hand eagerly. "I appreciate you coming up, Doc."

Dr. Taylor patted Thomas on his back, "it's my pleasure Thomas. See to it that your wife gets some rest now. Tomorrow I'll pop in to check on her for a routine visit. She's quite stable."

Bloneva stood with the doctor's coat in hand, ready to escort him to the door. She had heard Dr. Taylor give Jenny some general instructions, and she was eager to get back and assist. By the time Bloneva had returned to the room, Jenny was already nursing little Cassie, who seemed quite content as she nestled close to her mother.

Jenny stroked Cassie's cheek whenever she seemed to have stopped sucking. Without even opening her eyes, Cassie grinned radiantly and began drawing her mother's nourishment once more. Thomas was intrigued by his daughters' presence. He had already taken off his jacket and tie and sat on the edge of the bed watching his wife and child. Bloneva backed from the room, slowly closing the door, not wanting to intrude on their moment. Instead, she returned to the kitchen where she had begun their supper several hours before.

That was just about ten years ago. The thought of the entire day remained vivid in Bloneva's mind as though it had been only yesterday.

"My, my," Bloneva thought to herself, "I do believe I see why Ms. Jenny is so aggravated lately."

Bloneva tugged at a handful of Cassie's braids, indicating that her hair was done. Cassie stood to her feet and ambled away from her housekeeper.

"Excuse me, young lady," Bloneva called behind the little girl, her arms folded before her.

Cassie turned and smiled at Bloneva, "Yes, ma'am," she said, mocking her.

Bloneva's smile left her face. "Don't you forget your manners now, little Missy. I came in here to help you."

Cassie ran to Bloneva and threw her arms around their faithful housekeeper. "Thanks, Ms. Bloneva," she mumbled.

As Cassie strolled out from the room, Bloneva reached for the comb and brush and tidied the room.

"Ms. Jenny must have another little bun in the oven," she reasoned. She figured it must be something of that nature because of the way her boss had been acting recently. "Well, even so," she chided herself, "it really ain't my biz'ness until Ms. Jenny makes it so."

The thought of another baby in the house thrilled Bloneva. If Cassie had someone to play with or at least occupy her time, she would be less likely to get into so much mischief. Bloneva peeped on the back porch where she heard voices. Despite Ms. Jenny's threatening, she had Cassie all cuddled up to her, just talking and kissing her little girl on the forehead.

"I don't mean to get in scuffles, Mama," she heard Cassie explain to her mother. "It's just that if I'm going by Ike's or down by the docks to do a little fishing, someone almost always tries to meddle with me."

Jenny understood well, though she didn't care to inform her daughter of her childhood scrimmages just yet.

"Sweetie, I want you to try this for your mama, huh." Cassie looked intently at Jenny.

"What, Mama?"

Jenny pulled her daughter closer. "Try walking away from their teasing. Although you are a pretty strong little girl, there will always be more power at your disposal through the kindness of your words than by wielding your fists."

Cassie wasn't sure she agreed with her mother—she saw first-hand the respect she got when she instilled fear into her tormentors.

"Okay, Mama," she said smiling, "I'll try it your way." The truth of the matter was she was only willing to comply now rather than have her bottom whacked for the third time in one week.

"Sweetheart, if you want to have friends, you have to be friendly. You can't continue to frighten the kids away."

Cassie shrugged her shoulders. Her dad had told her the same thing many times before. She knew that some of the kids wanted to be her friend but were afraid of her and of being bullied by the rest of the kids in the village.

Jenny had also convinced her that the bullies were not all that bad either; they were just insecure and envious of her family's lifestyle. That didn't amount to a hill of beans to the ten-year-old girl, though. Having all that she had meant nothing to her since she didn't have anyone to share it with. The center in the village was also recently updated with outdoor slides and swings, but that didn't matter to the kids, even though it was Jenny's idea and money that made it a reality. Cassie was still not one of them. She didn't fit in.

~Chapter Thirty-four~

"**Ooowee I just knew it,** I could almost feel it in my bones, Ma'am." Bloneva grabbed hold of her apron with delight as she shrieked. "This is wonderful news. Congratulations, Ms. Jenny."

Jenny was amused with Bloneva's response. The way she clapped her hands and danced around the kitchen for the rest of the day, you would have thought that she was about to have a baby. Since Jenny had calmed down considerably and not gained any noticeable weight since the thought first ambled across Bloneva's mind, she hadn't considered it much anymore.

Now Jenny was approaching her sixth month and figured she'd let Cassie and Bloneva in on their secret. Thomas was thrilled. He often joked that he would like them to have as many children as she could produce. After the first several months of her pregnancy with Cassie, Jenny wasn't sure she would consider having another child. The long waiting period in between appeared to have numbed some of her memories of her first pregnancy. Bloneva saw it in a totally different light. Little Cassie had brought so much joy to the family that it far outweighed the challenges of an uncomfortable pregnancy.

Considering Jenny and Thomas never thought much about God, Bloneva took it upon herself to teach Cassie about her God. Cassie would lie across her bed, listening to her housekeeper talk about her God and what He had done for her. On her ninth birthday, Bloneva gave Cassie a gift that she thought would impact her life forever, a small Bible of her own, filled with bright pictures. Every day Bloneva came to work, Cassie had a bundle of questions for her. She was intrigued that there was someone all around her who had made everything and everyone and knew everything. Bloneva remembered how intrigued Cassie was when she explained how she could talk to God.

"He's the only one who is always available for us to talk to," Bloneva told the child. "It's like having a best friend who you can share all of your thoughts at any time, day or night. And," she paused, driving her point home. "He wants what's best for you and will never lead you astray."

Cassie perked up. Heaps of thoughts seemed to form at one time in her busy mind.

"That sounds awfully strange, but I kinda know what you mean. It's just that it doesn't always work out that way with me." Bloneva listened to the child patiently. "I sometimes say things because that's the way I want them to be. But most of the time, it doesn't happen the way I want it to, even when I really want it to so so much. Then, in the end, I come out looking silly."

Bloneva took Cassie's hand. "Listen, Cassandra Ford, if you read your Bible and talk to Him every day, you'll be amazed at the wonderful things He will begin to teach and give you."

"Ms. Bloneva, do you think God knows what I want?" Cassie probed.

"Yes, He knows what you want, Child, and more than that, He wants to give you everything that is good for you."

Cassie pressed further, "Ms. Bloneva, do you know what I really, really want?" Bloneva looked at the youngster quizzically.

"What could you want, Child? If I didn't know better, I would have bet you had everything a little girl could ever want!"

Her dad had an outdoor pool constructed for her with winding slides and waterfalls. She had three dogs she loved, a cat and a parrot that seemed to talk just as much as she did. Thomas even had one guest bedroom converted into a playroom with all the latest computerized games and a theater-style television.

"Uh, uh," Cassie shook her head, denying Bloneva's statement. "Ms. Bloneva, I want Mama to have a baby." Cassie sat up in the bed excitedly. "I sure would like to have someone to play with besides you, although you are a lot of fun," she added cautiously. "And even if me and God become best friends, He still won't come by and ride bicycles with me. He's probably a little older than you, and you won't ride with me."

Bloneva leaned over to the child and ruffled her hair. "I understand, Child. But why don't we just ask God to give you someone to play with?"

Cassie flopped back onto the bed dramatically, causing the pillows and her collection of stuffed toys to be scattered across the bed.

"I don't mean that kind of playmate. Ever since I stopped fighting in the village, Chase and Jasmine play with me sometimes when they're not listening to tattle tales about me. But I mean, I want a little brother or a sister." Cassie looked up from the bundle of curls that had escaped her ribbon and dangled loosely across her face. "Do you see what I mean? Anyway, you always have something good to tell me about your God answering your prayers. I was kinda wondering if you would say a special prayer for me to have a little sister."

Cassie, like her mom, was growing up to be a lonely child. She had all the treasures Thomas' money could buy but still sought after the simple things in life. A brother or sister, a fishing pole, her favorite worn-out jeans, and an old tape player Ike had given her on one of her visits to the village.

Now it was almost two years later that little Cassie's prayer was being answered. Her mother was going to have a baby in less than three months. Jenny still didn't understand why her housekeeper was so jubilant, but Cassie did. Still, Cassie had wondered whether God had really heard her prayer and if He did why the baby was so long in coming. Cassie didn't understand many things, but Bloneva encouraged her to continue reading and talking with the God of the Bible.

~Chapter Thirty-five~

There was a loud knock at the door. Jenny waddled towards the sound, hoping it wouldn't wake her daughter. The infant in her womb thumped energetically,

"Okay, sweet baby," she said softly, gently stroking her stomach. Her baby's movement seemed to have escalated somewhat in the past several hours. Normally Jenny would have been sleeping at this hour, but her infants' restlessness and Thomas' late arrival kept her up.

The knocking at the door increased. Perhaps Thomas had forgotten his house key again. His early mornings and late nights recently had put him into somewhat of a tailspin. Thomas was working long and hard to seal a refinancing deal for his resort. He was determined to be home with his family when Jenny gave birth to their second child. Jenny peered through the glass on the side of the door before attempting to open it.

"Mrs. Ford?" called a gentleman from the front porch. Jenny opened the door guardedly, not recognizing the voice but seeing that he was dressed in a policeman's uniform.

"I'm Mrs. Ford. What can I do for you?" The corporal moved his hat from his head and looked at his partner before addressing her again.

"I'm Corporal Reckly, and this is my partner Corporal Grant." The officer gazed at her blankly for a moment, not expecting to meet a pregnant woman. "May we come in for a moment?"

It was well past eleven o'clock. An odd time to make a house call, but Jenny was gracious nonetheless.

"Please do. What can I help you with?"

"It's your husband, Ma'am. I'm afraid his car skidded off the perimeter road. Apparently, there was a small oil spill that had not yet been cleaned up, the road was dark...Ma'am, the remains of his convertible was fished out of the ocean an hour ago. The search for his body has been called off for the time being on account of the weather and the fact that there is insufficient light in the area."

Jenny stumbled to a nearby chair, unable to grasp what she was hearing. The room felt as though it was whirling one way and her stomach the next. When she finally came to, the officers were standing over her calling her name. Jenny shook fiercely as she recalled their last statement to her. It couldn't be so, not her Thomas. Thomas, of all people, knew the danger of that road well. He was a good and cautious driver. Tears streamed uncontrollably down Jenny's face. This was utter madness. Her days of terror were behind her. She and Thomas had their whole lives ahead of them.

Bloneva came running through the door panting.

"Ms. Jenny," she cried. Her eyes were as wide as a flashlight. "I came as soon as I heard. Don't you worry, Ms. Jenny, we're gonna find Mr. Thomas and bring him back safe." Jenny held onto her housekeeper and wept. "Ike is rounding up some folks now. They say they're goin' out to check the water for themselves before he's swept off in the current. By morning it just might be too late."

A jolt of pain seared through Jenny's stomach, causing her to cry out in pain.

"Oh, not now," she cried, "I can't handle this right now." Corporal Grant took Jenny's hand. His wife had just had a baby three weeks before he was transferred to Maruba.

"Take your time Ma'am," he coached her. "Breathe easy, that's it. Everything is gonna be jus' alright." Jennifer tried to regain her composure for the sake of her baby, but it was difficult.

"Ma'am, my partner and I will take you to the clinic. If you would get your bag, we can take you now."

Fresh warm tears swathed Jenny's cheeks. Thomas had promised to be here for this moment. Now he may never even see his child at all.

"Ms. Jenny, I'll stay with Cassie. You go along. Everything will be jus' alright. Soon as we're able," she said, attempting to smile, "we'll be right at your bedside."

Bloneva gave the officers Jenny's packed bag that was in the hallway closet. "You all drive carefully now and call me when you get there safe."

At the crack of dawn Bloneva was up and had breakfast prepared for Cassie.

"Come, Child," she roused her gently from her sleep. "We going to see your mama. Maybe we can get you all fixed up and pretty 'cause she might have a surprise for us."

Cassie was always one for surprises. She bolted out of her bed, showered within minutes, ate her breakfast, and made herself ready to see her mother. Bloneva skirted down the winding path towards the clinic in her noisy yellow Volkswagen. Considering the horrid weather, which passed over briefly last night, it was a gorgeous day. The small car sputtered into the pebbled driveway of the clinic. An elderly nurse greeted them at the door smiling.

"Your mama is doing fine, little girl," she said to Cassie, allaying Bloneva's fears. "And by the way, you have a beautifully healthy, bouncing baby brother."

Bloneva took Cassie's hand and squeezed it. "How about we go for a quick look-see?" Cassie ran down the corridor of the little clinic, looking through each door for her mother.

The nurse took Bloneva's hand and pulled her to the side. "It was quite a close call for Ms. Ford. The doctor will be releasing her when he returns, but she must remain calm for her sake and the baby's. We almost lost the little fellow, but he is quite a fighter. Please try to keep her calm when you talk with her. It has been a difficult session."

~Chapter Thirty-six~

Days turned into weeks as Jenny awaited some word on her husband. Ike and his friends found nothing as they scoured the coast for signs of Thomas' body. 'The baby,' as everyone called him, grew stronger every day. He was a pleasant, easy-going child, not at all as demanding as his sister had been.

Bloneva spent most of her days and evenings on Ford Hill, not wanting to leave Jenny or the children by themselves. They were trying to cope the best they could, but somehow not finding Thomas' body was taking its toll.

"Ms. Jenny," Bloneva approached her one day. "You are alive. You have two beautiful children who are also alive and well. You have much to be thankful for. Your children need you, Ma'am," she whispered to her employer.

It seemed that all Jenny could do and had been doing for the past month was to cry. The thought of facing the world without Thomas was bleak. "I know, Bloneva, but I just don't know what to do. I feel so helpless. The only person I ever had to turn to was Thomas, and now I don't have him."

Bloneva pointed to the baby that lay sleeping in the cradle near the bed. "You have a part of him. This little boy is the image of his daddy, and he and Cassie need you now more than ever."

Jenny looked at her sweet child as he slept comfortably. "I don't know what to do. What should I do?" she asked, pulling the covers up to her neck.

"Well, for starters, you need to get out of this bed. Open the curtains and breathe in this good life God has given you. And for heaven's sake, Ma'am, you need to name your child!"

Jenny pulled herself up and out of her bed that had been her sanctuary since her return home. "Bloneva, please help me. You are so strong. I need your help."

Bloneva nodded. "Yes, Ma'am, I'll help you. But what if I'm not here? Who would you rely on then? I think it's high time you met my God. He will be your strength when you are weak, and He promises to be your comforter."

Bloneva knew firsthand what she was telling Jenny to be true. It was only through facing the challenges in her life that she became strong. At one time, she thought it would have been easier to crawl up a dark hole and die, but that wouldn't have solved her problem. In fact, as she well knew, it would have created more lasting problems for her young family. Having tried many avenues of advice and counsel, only her faith in the good Lord brought her through.

"The only way folks make it through a storm alive and in one piece, Ma'am, is getting on their knees and asking God for His help," she told her employer solemnly. "If you don't bow now, you will break later."

Bloneva pulled back the curtains and stood gaping out the window, her hands akimbo.

"Look here, Ma'am, now ain't that a beautiful sight? Some folks didn't wake up this mornin' to see such a beautiful day. You've gotta give God thanks, Ms. Jenny," Bloneva said, shaking her head as she picked up Cassie's slipper from the floor.

The only time Jenny recalled really listening to anyone talk about God was on her wedding day and of course the few times she overheard Cassie asking Bloneva questions. But for the most part, she had not factored God into her life. Jenny recalled the old preacher handing them his Bible as he spoke of his God with such love and assurance at their wedding. She reached for the Bible they had kept in the nightstand untouched for so many years.

"That's right, Ma'am," Bloneva encouraged her, "everything you need is right in the pages of that same book. You can start by reading the book of Psalms, it'll give you peace."

Bloneva closed the door behind her; she knew her boss was going to be just all right. She walked into the kitchen to check on Cassie, who was busy sampling the cookie batter they had mixed minutes before. The child was still a trite somber but was coming along quite well.

"How about us goin' for a walk in the village, Cassie?" Bloneva asked excitedly. Cassie shrugged her shoulders. She had spent most of her day in her father's study looking through his photos and missing him a great deal.

~Chapter Thirty-seven~

Bianca Winthroppe lay sprawled on the deck of her father's yacht. Her short red hair was ablaze in the sun as she flicked through a stack of architectural magazines. She was bored and lonely. As usual, her parents were away on a business trip, which left her with much time on her hands. At twenty-two and sole heir to the family's fortune, Bianca led an overly protected life. Notwithstanding her family's fortune attracted a myriad of suitors, many of whom were equally well off, neither they nor Winthroppe Aviation managed to keep her attention for any particular length of time.

It wasn't until the day her crew spotted a man adrift on a large tree branch alongside her anchored yacht after a passing squall, did she feel some glimmer of excitement. Though partially alert and able to stay afloat, he had no recollection of how he got there or how long he had been in the water.

In spite of their cautioning, Bianca chose to nurse the battered young man back to health. For several months he stayed on board, struggling to regain his memory and strength. Almost five weeks later, the handsome stranger was beginning to mend nicely, the gashes to his body virtually disappearing as the days elapsed. His biggest struggle, it seemed, was regaining his memory. An attainment Bianca would have preferred to dispose of.

For their ease in communication, Bianca called her guest Tad. Tad had apparently no other form of identification on him except a rather attractive gold watch that bore the initials T. F. Despite his preoccupation with regaining his memory and the jolts of pain that seared through his head on occasion, Bianca found her guest to be attentive, kind and seemingly unimpressed with the luxury that surrounded him. For that reason alone, Bianca was attracted to him. It wasn't long before Bianca felt herself falling in love with Tad, who had no particular interest in the stunning beauty.

In their travels through the islands, a rumor surfaced among the crew of a missing man in the area. Without much speculation, the crew decided that Tad was in all probability the missing man. He did, after all, fit the description. From the time it was said that an accident had occurred on the little island to the short period Tad's body washed against their vessel, seemed confirmation enough to the avid crew who were bent on solving the mystery of the missing man.

Their findings were not at all welcomed by their employer, who threatened her crew should they have any foolish notions of informing her guest or anyone else of their ill-founded rumors. From that time on, Bianca had her captain remain on the open water far from any of the islands. Not long after, Bianca's expressions towards Tad became more distinct.

"Tad, you don't know who you are, and I don't care who you are. All I know is that you have become quite special to me."

Bianca inched her way seductively towards Tad. Though quite flattered by the young red-haired beauty, Tad was not inclined to follow her leading, though it had been quite tempting at times.

"I appreciate your kindness to me, but if I do have a family they will be waiting for me and extremely worried. I must find out my identity."

Bianca pouted, seeing that her manipulative ploys were not being effective with her latest conquest.

146

"I keep having flashes of voices and faces, Bianca. Though I must admit they are not connecting, I'm sure with time, all the pieces will fit neatly together."

Secretly Bianca was hoping the opposite. If Tad never regained his memory, she had a greater chance of winning his affection.

"You're quite confident, aren't you, Tad? With me, you have an opportunity to start all over again. I have enough money to take care of us for the rest of our lives."

Tad rubbed his eyes warily for a moment and reclined on the lounge chair. Within seconds Bianca was beside him attempting to lavish him with her affections. Overwhelmed, Tad embraced her and responded to her kisses.

"Oh Tad, I love you," she sighed.

"Bianca, I'm sorry. You are beautiful, charming, and any man who doesn't find you desirable would be blind." Tad got up from the chair and began to walk towards the door. "I can't explain it, but I know I have a family. I can sometimes hear a child's voice calling for me. I must find them, Bianca, and I will."

Bianca attempted to reason with Tad, "But what if, what if you are a fugitive?" Tad smiled and pointed his finger at her, "Then, my friend, you ought to be more careful picking up strangers and keeping them hostage in the middle of the ocean."

Bianca was outraged "Is that what you think I am doing, holding you hostage? You are free to leave whenever you wish."

Thomas scratched his head. "I don't mean to seem ungrateful; I appreciate you and your crew saving my life. But I need to know where you rescued me from and have you deliver me to the closest inhabited land to that point. When I am able, I assure you, I will repay you for your kindness."

~Chapter Thirty-eight~

The sun had begun to set, and it was a beautiful evening. Bloneva had left early to look after some personal business, excusing herself from Jenny and the children. Jenny was making a great effort to take charge of her life. Within the past few weeks, she was beginning to blossom once again. Cassie was singing and smiling, and music filled the house for the first time in months.

A stranger to Ford Hill, Bianca pulled up the driveway in a rental van. She sat quietly for a moment, not sure she could go through with her plans. Following the leads she had gotten from her crew, she was determined to talk with the missing man's family. Taking a deep breath, Bianca climbed from the vehicle and walked briskly to the front door. Just as she was about to knock on the door, Cassie bolted out with her cat in hand, almost crushing their visitor on the porch.

"Oh dear," she exclaimed, "I'm sorry I didn't expect anyone to be out here. I just wanted to get Kitty outside before my mom found her in the kitchen again."

The stranger giggled at the charming little girl as she scrambled to her feet. Bianca extended her hand to Cassie.

"Are your parents home?"

Cassie shook her head, "Hi, I'm Cassie. Do you want to see my mom?" Cassie took the stranger's hand and led her into their home.

"Well, it's a pleasure to meet you, Cassie. I'm Bianca. And if your mom is available, I'd love to see her for a moment."

"Your hair is so cool, Bianca!" she exclaimed as her new friend walked inside. "It looks like my favorite vegetables!"

Bianca laughed. The child was so sweet. She seemed to have bundles of energy too. "I guess your favorite vegetable is carrot."

Bianca gazed around the room, hoping not to find what she was looking for. Her fears were confirmed as she picked up a framed photograph of Cassie and her parents.

"Hullo, my daughter told me that someone was out here to see me. I'm sorry I didn't hear the doorbell." Bianca returned the photo to the entry table before turning to meet Jenny.

"I apologize for springing on you like this, but I'm lost and was hoping you could direct me to Northern Springs," she sputtered a lame excuse for finding her way inside Tad's home.

She was hoping not to find his home or find one he would not be too eager to return to. But that was not the case. Jenny cradled baby Thomas in her arms, rocking him gently as she gave Bianca the directions.

Bianca sat in the van for a moment, overwhelmed with disappointment. She knew now she had to let Tad know who he really was. It was unavoidable. He would find out somehow anyway. Tad had a lovely family. Even with his loss of memory, he had a connection so strong, bonding him with them. Bianca figured his name must have been Thomas after hearing Cassie call the baby's name as she tugged at her brother's sock. That would account for the initials on the back of his watch.

Tad was right about her holding him hostage. Bianca wept shamelessly inside the van. What had she come to? When she wasn't paying people to travel with her, she was keeping them against their will. She had everything, yet she had nothing. Her life was beginning to look like someone she knew who paid people to be her friend. Bianca started the van and reversed down the hill.

"By tomorrow," she promised herself, "Tad would be reunited with his family."

As the skiff was being retrieved from the water, Bianca scanned the boat's deck for Tad. After further thought, she knew that she had to apologize to him right away and have one of her crews return him to his family. A young deck hand approached her cautiously, guessing that it was Tad she was looking for.

"Ma'am, I'm afraid he's gone. There was nothing we could do," he said, looking at his employer with his head cast to the side.

"What do you mean, he's gone!" Bianca shrieked at her staff, clinging to the rail of the vessel. "How did he leave if I had the speed boat?" The men all started to explain at the same time. Bianca held her head as she dramatized her point. "He's a sick man. He will never make it to the island alive. Relaunch the boat, and don't return until you've found him." She strode off to the open bridge, hoping to sight him with her binoculars.

"Ma'am, I'm afraid these won't help you any," the yacht's captain took the binoculars from Bianca and placed them in a compartment. "Tad left shortly after you did this morning. He overheard the crew telling you of the missing man in the village and where to go to find his family. There was nothing we could do to stop him." He turned back to Bianca, "he also knew that we would be leaving the area this evening due to an approaching cold front.

"Captain, I hope you know that I was only trying to help him the best way I know how," Bianca whimpered, hoping to win some support.

"I'm sure you were, Ma'am. But he's a man. With or without his full memory, you must realize that Tad, as you call him, is a man. You cannot lead him, nor can you make him into something he isn't."

Bianca watched as several of her men boarded the skiff. They had two hours to search the area before the captain pulled out of the area. It was well past five o'clock. If he were a strong swimmer, he would have reached the shore by now. If not, Tad was shark bait.

~Chapter Thirty-nine~

"I jus' feel like I'm gonna make** a big catch today," mulled Bobo as he repositioned himself on his favorite spot on the rock.

Bobo was a big boy for his age. Although he was only twelve years old, he was known for his size and his appetite. His real name was Robert Smith, but his friends called him Bobo on account of his bubble shape.

Bobo's fishing mates Manny and Ziggy giggled to themselves. That was Bobo's talk every time they went fishing and every time he came up empty-handed, claiming part of their catch as his own.

"Y'all jus' wait and see. One of these days, I'm gonna pull in a big one."

The boys sat quietly for a while, hoping that there would be a great catch today. The point had been their favorite fishing grounds from as far back as they could remember. It didn't matter much that today the sky was somewhat overcast; most of their time was spent expanding their old fish tales and talking about the prettiest girls in the village. Girls like Cassie Ford. She was pretty all right, but everyone knew that "Miss Hot-head Cassie" was not interested in boys yet. Lately, she wasn't even interested in herself. But that didn't stop Manny from dreaming.

"Whas that out there, man?" Bobo inquired as he pulled in his line. "I'm sure thas a big one. That baby is mine!" he exclaimed proudly to his friends as he swung his line in the direction of the stirring water. Manny jumped up to see what his friend was talking about.

"Bobo, either you are dense or blind. Can't you see that's someone out there swimmin'?"

Bobo reached into his shirt pocket for his glasses as his friends dropped their lines and darted across the rocks to the other side of their fishing grounds. Manny was the first to reach the area.

"It's a white man," he shouted to his friends. "Ziggy, go get some help. I think he looks like Mr. Ford."

Manny and Bobo jumped in the water to where Thomas was swimming. He looked as though he could barely lift his arms another stroke as he awkwardly kicked his way to the rocks.

"We've got you, Mr. Ford," Bobo shouted as they pulled Thomas to shore.

Thomas rolled over on his back and gasped for air. He felt the warm sand beneath him as he rubbed his hand across the surface.

"Mr. Ford, you sure had us worried. Everyone thought you was dead," Manny told him guardedly.

Bobo wasn't quite as cautious. "Hmph, everyone except his hot-tempered daughter Cassie."

Bobo was oblivious to the harsh look Manny was sending his way.

"Anyone who mentioned that you was dead had to reckon with her. I don't know why that little girl like to fight so!"

Manny rolled his eyes at his friend. Now he had removed all doubt and proved his point. Bobo was undeniably dense.

It was all coming back to Thomas now. He was beginning to put the pictures of his mind together with the voices and names that he had been hearing for the past month or so. Thomas propped himself up on his elbows.

"Thank you, boys. I appreciate your help," he said, barely able to whisper.

"Don't thank us yet sir, we ain't taken you home yet. Ooh ... when Ms. Jenny sees you, and that big pretty smile spread cross her face, thas all the thanks we gonna need."

Fortunately for Thomas, Blake Smith was driving by as Ziggy ran down the road hysterically, trying to get the attention of a passing vehicle. Blake could hardly believe his eyes when he saw Thomas struggling up the path to the roadside, barely able to walk. Thomas was a sight for sore eyes. Without much thought, Blake quickly ran towards Thomas, his burly frame unhindered by the bushes that were scattered on the rocky path. He quickly propped Thomas up and carried him with little effort to his car.

~Chapter Forty~

enny sat on the back porch reading to Cassie, neither of them particularly interested in the story, yet still attempting to please the other.

"Thanks, Mama," Cassie told her mother politely. I think I'm going to look at daddy's photo album again."

Jenny could hardly hold back the tears. Her little girl had been so strong and determined throughout the whole ordeal. She was convinced her daddy was coming back to them, and nothing Jenny could say to her would ever change that.

"Okay, Sweetheart," Jenny answered, "but when you're finished, I want you to clean up the toys you left on the floor before you do anything else."

Cassie slid off the patio chair and gave her mom a hug, "Yes, Ma'am," she said, giving Jenny a half smile.

"Cass," Jenny called after her, "Mama is so proud of you, and I love you very much."

Cassie nodded as she held onto the porch door, "I know, Mama," she said, tears beginning to stream down her face, "I love you too."

It was shortly after seven o'clock when Blake dropped Thomas off at his house. Thomas sat staring at the structure for a few minutes before staggering out of the vehicle. He reached over to Blake and shook his hand. Though he felt weak and somewhat disoriented, he wanted to be alone with his family.

"I appreciate your help, man. If you don't mind, I'd like to take it from here."

Blake nodded his head and smiled. There was something different about Thomas, but he figured there would be something different about him too if he plunged from the road into the ocean and went missing for almost three and a half months.

"Take it easy, Thomas, and welcome back. We all missed you."

Blake shifted his gear to neutral as he rolled down the hill, hoping to jump-start his old car on the way down. Instead of knocking on the front door, Thomas held onto the railing while making his way up the steps and around to the back porch where he and Jenny had spent many of their evenings. Jenny sat deep in thought, not hearing her husband's footsteps as he made his way toward her.

"Jenny," he said, treading wearily, his clothing still saturated with salt water. Jenny looked up, wiping her eyes. She didn't expect any visitors at all and hoped they didn't see her crying. When Thomas came closer, Jenny stood up and ran to him, almost toppling him over.

"Oh my," she cried, "oh Thomas, Thomas is it really you?" Thomas held his wife tightly, tears flowing from both their eyes as they smiled and laughed and kissed each other. "If this is another dream, Thomas, I don't ever want to wake up."

Thomas wiped the tears from Jenny's eyes.

"This is no dream, Jenny. Our nightmare is behind us." Jenny stepped back from Thomas to take another look at him.

"How I missed you," she said, rubbing her hands up and down his arms. "Darling, you're wet," Jenny noted.

"I know, Sweetheart, but I'm fine." Memories of their past flooded Thomas' mind. He looked around for his daughter, "Jenny, how are you? Where's Cassie? How is she?"

Jenny took her husband by the hand and led him to his study where Cassie had spent much of her time since his disappearance.

"We're all doing pretty good, Thomas, but how are you, my love? It's so good to have you home."

Cassie had fallen asleep on her father's leather sofa, with her favorite family photo album across her chest. Thomas gently lifted the album from his daughter's grasp without waking her. He kissed her lightly on the forehead and followed his wife out of the room.

"I'd like to wash up, Jen, and get out of these clothes. Then we can talk some more," he explained, peeling his wet shirt from his back. "I want to know everything that has happened since I last saw you."

Every fiber of Thomas' body ached. He was exhausted. "Perhaps after a cool shower, his head would quit thumping," he thought.

As Jenny walked towards the kitchen to prepare a light snack for her husband, she clasped her hands to her chest and whispered a thank you prayer. Thomas was home. He looked a bit disoriented and disheveled, much like what she had felt for the past several months, but he was back in one piece, and she was thankful. Thomas took a quick shower and lay across his bed. Moments later, he was fast asleep.

Jenny checked on little Thomas in the nursery before lifting Cassie to her room and putting her to bed. Tomorrow the kids would be reunited with their father. She could hardly wait to see the look on Cassie's face when she woke up in the morning.

Tonight would be an early night for everyone. Jenny stretched out on the side of her husband, stroking his head and nestling against him before she too fell asleep with a smile of contentment across her face.

~Chapter Forty-one~

"**D**addy, Daddy, Daddy!" **Cassie** shouted excitedly as she noticed her father strewn across the bed, still deep in his sleep.

Jenny smiled at her daughter as she plunged on the bed just as she had done many times in the past, squeezing between the two of them. Thomas turned over slowly. It was a joy to see his daughter again.

"I knew you would come back to us, Daddy," she said quietly as she hugged him tighter.

"Let me take a look at you, Princess. My, you have grown and oh, so pretty too!" Thomas sat up and placed his daughter in front of him, kissing her from cheek to cheek. "So, young lady, we have a lot of talking to catch up on."

Cassie shook her head excitedly. She loved her mom so, but her daddy held a special place in her heart. He knew just how to spoil her, something her mother never quite mastered. Thomas winced slightly as he stood up. The shooting pain he had experienced as a result of the accident felt like volts of electricity through his head.

"Are you okay, Daddy?" Cassie inquired, concerned by the look on her father's face.

"You betcha, kid," he answered, pulling on two of her braids at either side of her head. "I'm just going to freshen up so that we can sit out on the back porch and have a nice chat like we used to." Cassie smiled. "Maybe you can show me how you've progressed with your swimming too!" he added.

Little Thomas whimpered just as his daddy walked into the shower.

"Mama," Cassie whispered to Jenny, "has daddy seen T. J. yet?" Jenny shook her head.

"No baby, not yet. Let's get the little tiger and introduce him to his daddy."

When Cassie walked into her little brother's room, his face lit up with smiles.

"I love you too, little brother," she said, leaning over the crib and rubbing his soft tummy.

Cassie continued to entertain her brother as Jenny changed his diaper and sat him up in the corner of the crib.

"Well, look at my big boy," she said proudly. "Are you ready to meet your daddy, precious boy?" Jenny extended her hands to her son, who appeared more than eager to be held by his mother.

Thomas' face paled for a moment at the shock of seeing his son. He had completely forgotten that his wife was pregnant.

"You look like you've just seen a ghost, Thomas," Jenny whispered, handing Thomas their baby.

"He's beautiful, Jen," he said, embracing his son.

So much had happened in the past several months Jenny knew she had to give Thomas some time to regroup and reestablish himself. Right now, he looked much like a fish out of water. She had many questions for her husband. Cassie was not as patient as her mother. Waiting was not a luxury she cared to embrace. For three and a half months, she languished over her father. Now that he had returned, she expected his full and undivided attention.

"Where were you, Daddy, and why didn't you call us?" she said, snuggling closer to him. "Everybody thought you were dead, but not me. I knew you wouldn't leave me without saying goodbye."

Thomas couldn't get a word in edgeways. He looked at his wife who appeared to be just as eager as their daughter in hearing the answer to her questions.

"I suppose now is about as good a time as any to tell you what happened. Thomas handed his son back to Jenny. "I'm not exactly sure what happened the night of my accident. I simply haven't been able to remember it. But from what I heard, there was an accident... my car plunged down the ridge into the ocean."

Thomas pressed his fingers against his eyes, trying to recall the sequence of events.

"I must have been thrown out of the car and into the ocean because at some point I was being fished out of the water by an anchored yacht."

Jenny's brow furrowed as her husband rehashed his ordeal.

"Apparently, I could not remember who I was or where I'd come from. The people on board nursed me back to health. I'm told I was pretty bruised up." Thomas noticed the concern on both Cassie's and Jenny's faces as he spoke.

"I probably looked a lot worse than I was," he reassured them. "I started to regain my memory in bits and pieces, and then one day, I overheard the crew talking. They heard of a missing person on the island that fit my description."

Thomas sighed, "I knew that it would be my last opportunity to find out if this was the island I had come from, as we were scheduled to leave the area later that day. As someone had already taken the dory out, I was left no other option but to swim to shore and find my family for myself."

As Thomas spoke, both Jenny's and Cassie's eyes were filled with tears. They were sorry that he had encountered so much. Jenny knew now why Thomas was surprised to see his son. Thomas held his family's hands.

"It's good to be home. Though I couldn't remember details, I was sure that I had a loving family waiting for me somewhere."

Now it was Jenny's time to ask a few questions. "Why didn't the folks on the yacht bring you back to the nearest island where they had found you?"

Thomas shrugged his shoulders.

"I would have thought," she continued matter-of-factly, "that it would've been an automatic thing to contact the authorities in the area and alert them of their findings." Thomas agreed with his wife. "Well, perhaps Thomas, you would care to tell me then, the part of this story you are intentionally omitting."

Thomas turned to Cassie and tweaked her nose.

"How about getting your dad a tall glass of juice, Princess," he requested, hoping for a few moments of privacy with his wife.

"Sure Dad," Cassie sulked, knowing he was trying to get rid of her. Cassie walked away and closed the door behind her, leaving it slightly ajar.

"Jenny, the person who saved my life was a woman. She nursed me back to health. I believe she became a little attached to me and intentionally kept me from returning home."

Jenny set little T. J. on the floor to play.

"And you; did you become attached to her too, Thomas?" she asked, not sure what she might hear next.

"No Jenny, Bianca was no interest to me at all. She was kind and generous, and I'll never forget her saving my life. But I chose to come home; I chose to be reunited with my family."

Just as Jenny was about to embrace her husband, Cassie bolted in.

"Did you say, Bianca, Dad?" Thomas and Jenny looked at their daughter, wondering how long she had been listening. "Mama," Cassie continued, "remember the lady who came by yesterday. You know, the one with the carrot-colored hair? Well, she said her name was Bianca too!"

Thomas knew that Bianca had taken the dory and was up to something, but he was surprised to hear that she had paid his family a visit. She had obviously known where he lived. Thomas turned to his wife and daughter, a faint smile managing to crease his lips.

"If you don't mind, ladies," he said gently, "I would like to put the whole ordeal behind me. I've missed enough time away from you already." Jenny squeezed her husband's hand and kissed him briskly.

"I'm going to prepare you a hearty breakfast, Sweetheart. I'm sure Cassie will keep you occupied for a while."

Cassie could think of nothing better that she would love to do. Spending time with her dad was just about all that occupied her mind for the past few months. By the end of breakfast, the whole island was aware of Thomas' return. Versions of his absence reached frenzied proportions.

For the first time in the history of their native island paradise, the police department was alerted to an apparent kidnapping. For some, it was the pinnacle of their existence on the island. For so long, the police were called in for minor infractions to the law, like when Bobo and his friends raided Ms. Stubbs pineapple field. They sat for hours, filing down every juicy pineapple in sight.

Now that was the talk of the town! True to form, their underworked crime unit swooped in and apprehended the assailants. For the next several weeks, the trio worked in Ms. Stubbs' field, cleaning and harvesting her fruit until they were sick of seeing pineapples.

Fortunately, for the undermanned police department, Thomas was not interested in pressing charges against Bianca and her crew. Although his stay on the yacht was lengthy, he was appreciative of their help in keeping him alive.

~Chapter Forty-two~

Everything on Ford Hill seemed to be getting back to normal as Thomas spent all of his time recuperating from his recent ordeal. Neither Thomas nor Jenny had paid much attention to the affairs of the resort until the news of foreclosure came crashing into their world. Before the accident, Thomas' attitude would have been to fight to regain control of his life's work. Now he had resigned himself to the loss, not having the physical or mental strength to do anything about it.

"There's nothing, absolutely nothing I can do about it now, Jen," he confided apologetically to his wife. "I've read over the documents, and from what I can see, fighting would only prolong the inevitable and drain us of the savings that we do have."

Jenny felt like a part of her had been crushed. She knew what the resort had meant to Thomas and felt as though she was grieving the loss of a child.

"I'm still young, Jen, and so are you. All is not lost. We still have each other and a bright future before us."

Jenny appreciated her husband's consolation. She had always relied heavily upon his guidance. Had it not been for the accident, the short-term loan Thomas had taken out to inject capital into the property would have turned itself over numerous times. It seemed that one hurdle was lined up after the next for Jenny and Thomas.

After insisting on Thomas visiting a neurological specialist on the mainland, it was determined that a massive clot had formed on his brain. The cause was due to the severe blow sustained to his head.

"We could go in and do some exploratory surgery and drain the blood at the same time," suggested Dr. Mallory. "But there are no guarantees of success. Since we aren't sure where the blood is coming from, we might just be irritating the situation more than we would care to."

The news was shocking to both Thomas and Jenny, as they had initially been told that he was suffering from a pinched nerve and severe stress, which would not only cause the pain in his head but would account for his bouts of disorientation.

"Dr. Mallory," Jenny asked, seeming to grasp the wind that was knocked from her, "what recourse do we have?"

"We're going to do all that we can, my dear, to get to the bottom of this. But it may take a few weeks." Dr. Mallory pulled up a stool and spun around to his desk as he reached for a pen in his pocket.

"I'm going to give you something, Thomas, to relieve the pain and reduce the inflammation. I want you to check back with me in a week. We'll take another scan and see if there is any improvement."

Thomas edged from his seat on the examination table gingerly as he took the prescription from his doctor.

"Thanks for your time," he said, shaking Dr. Mallory's hand briskly. "I'll see you in a week."

Dr. Mallory had seen many cases like this one in the past. Had Thomas received treatment earlier his chances would have been better. He would determine if the bleeding had escalated or had maintained its standing once Thomas got the necessary rest and completed his medication. Dr. Mallory wasn't sure at this point whether the pressure treatments for the pinched nerve diagnosis had actually helped or hindered his progress. What he did know was that if there was no improvement in a week, Thomas' chances of survival was slim.

~Chapter Forty-three~

Thomas was soon feeling more like himself but still not completely well. He and Cassie spent hours fishing and swimming and doing the things they had always done together in the past. Thomas had almost forgotten that he had an ailment. The painkillers he took did wonders for cloaking the symptoms. Even though Thomas wasn't particularly interested in going back to the doctor, he agreed to do so anyway, simply to allay his wife's concerns.

The trip to the mainland was a rigorous one. For many years Thomas had relied on his private aircraft for transportation to the mainland. Chartering a flight on a seaplane was the next best thing. Several mail boats were making frequent trips to the island for the past several years, but that mode of transportation was not considered by Thomas or Jenny.

The cool morning air was wonderfully refreshing as Thomas and Jenny made their way to the hospital. Both of them were engrossed in thought, not wanting to alarm the other of the possible outcome of the upcoming doctor's visit. Jenny contacted Gertie the moment she arrived at the hospital. The two had maintained a close relationship and kept in touch throughout Jenny's marriage and during her latest trial of Thomas' disappearance. Apart from Ike, Gertie was the only friend Jenny had to console her through her dark moments.

"I'm glad you came, Gertie." Jenny embraced her friend as tears rolled down her face. "I didn't know I had so many tears left in me," she quipped, attempting to make light of the moment.

"You'll both make it, Jen," Gertie encouraged her friend. "It's hard, I know. But if anyone is a survivor, I'd say it was you." Jenny wiped her eyes and thanked her friend.

"It gives me the shivers, Gertie, how much pain Thomas has been in for such a long time, and he hardly ever complained."

Gertie stayed with Jenny for most of the day, not once leaving the hospital compound.

"Are you sure I can't get you something to eat, Jen? You do look a bit drained."

Drained was not quite the word Jenny had in mind when she caught a glimpse of her reflection in the mirror.

"I guess I can use a cold glass of juice and one of those fluffy apple tarts I saw in the cafeteria earlier. I think I'll go and refresh my make-up before I'm mistaken for a wise old owl with all this smeared mascara around my eyes."

It was nearly four o'clock, and Gertie had to leave. She was great company for Jenny as usual. No matter how long the two of them had been apart, they always seemed to pick up as though they had just seen each other moments before.

"Give my love to Thomas, Jenny. I'm gonna be praying for the two of you," Gertie assured her friend.

"I know I can count on you, Gertie." Jenny waved at her friend as she walked briskly down the dimly lit corridor to the main entrance.

The day was long, and Thomas was tired. The tests seemed more painful than the affliction. Although, for the most part, Jenny was not permitted to be in the room with Thomas as he underwent a barrage of scans and blood tests, Thomas felt her presence near him. She had developed, it seemed, a peace about her that was of great comfort to him. Dr. Mallory's prognosis was grim. He had called several other specialists in to discuss their findings.

"We'd like to admit you today, Thomas. We believe we can help you if we can just get in there to see better. The good news is, the swelling has gone down a little, and your vital signs are strong enough for us to operate right away." Thomas was pleased that Jenny was not in the room with him to hear the doctors' findings.

"We believe," Dr. Mallory continued, "we may not have such an opportunity again, Thomas. With your permission, we would like to operate tomorrow morning."

Thomas was not impressed with his doctor's summation.

"You've probed, gouged, and scanned me in ways and places I never knew existed, and the best you can tell me is that you *believe* you can help me!" Thomas gathered his belongings and made his way to the door. "I'll give it some thought," he said, containing his anger, "but it won't be today or tomorrow."

Jenny waited patiently inside the visitor's lounge for her husband to complete his examinations. She felt a huge weight lifted from her shoulders as Thomas walked towards her. He wanted nothing more than to rest.

Thomas reached for his wife's hand. "Come, Sweetheart, let's go home."

Jenny looked at her husband, wanting to know each detail of his examination and the doctors' findings. Thomas knew his wife well. "We'll talk later, Jen. It's been a grueling day, but I'm going to make it."

Much to Dr. Mallory's regret, Thomas opted not to have the surgery. If it meant decreasing the quality of his life and with limited guarantees of success, he would continue taking the painkillers and spend the rest of his time with his family. For many nights, Jenny thrashed about in her bed, wondering if it would be her last night of seeing her husband alive. Thomas sought opinions from other doctors, who, for the most part, were in agreement with Dr. Mallory's diagnosis.

A hospital volunteer walked up to Thomas as he was leaving. "Sir," she said, attempting to get his attention, "please, I'd like you to have this."

It was a little pamphlet with a cross on the front. Thomas glanced at it before putting it in his pocket.

~Chapter Forty-four~

There were days when Thomas' strength waned, and Jenny thought he would take his last breath as he gasped for air. Since returning home, Thomas' medication virtually tripled in strength. He had reached the maximum dosage any doctor could prescribe for his painkiller. Even with considerable assistance from their insurance, Jenny noticed a sharp dent in their resources due to medical expenses.

As far as she was concerned, it didn't matter what the cost was. Jenny knew she would pay for his medication, with or without insurance. She simply could not bear to see him gripping his head as though the pressure inside was about to give way. It tore at Thomas to see how his declining health was affecting his wife.

"Come here, darling, sit with me awhile," he patted a spot on the bed for his wife to come near. "I'm so sorry for what I've put you through, my love. I would give you the world if I could." Jenny took her husband's hand and cupped it lovingly to her cheek.

"You have given me the world, Thomas Ford, and don't you ever forget it."

Thomas shifted his hands slowly as though his movements required great effort as he wiped away her tears.

"Don't cry, Sweetie. You have always been my love and will always be. I could not have asked for a better wife or a better mother for our children." Thomas smiled and closed his eyes for a while. "You know, Jen, you're just as beautiful now as the day we were married. I thought I would perish waiting for the ceremony to be over."

Jenny kissed her husband on his lips gently, his smile never leaving his face. Fresh tears flooded Jenny's face. She knew she was losing him. He had fought valiantly all his life, and continued even now.

"Thomas," she wept aloud. "Thomas, please don't leave me. Please, Thomas, I'll do anything. Tell me what to do, Sweetheart."

Thomas squeezed his wife's hand softly. He spoke to her gently, not wanting to arouse the pain he was feeling in his head. His words were becoming more slurred as he spoke.

"What haven't you done already, my love? You've made my life worth living for the past decade. You must continue to live, Jenny. You're a good woman, and you deserve the best."

Jenny knelt on the floor next to the bed, her hand wrapped around her husbands' chest. She felt sick to her stomach.

"Please God," she shouted, "please help my husband. Oh God, you can't let him die."

Cassie ran into her parents' room, hearing her crying from the moment she had walked in from school.

"What's the matter, Mama?" she said, bolting into the room. Cassie turned to her father, who was slipping away.

"Daddy," she whispered gently over his face. "Are you alright, Daddy?"

Thomas opened his eyes briefly and smiled at his daughter. "Hey, Princess, you're back early," he whispered. His eyes fluttered sporadically as he mustered the strength to talk to his daughter.

"Cass, you help Mama look after your brother, okay. Daddy loves you so, so much."

"Daddy," Cassie screamed as she squeezed her father's hand. "Daddy, you've only just come back home. You can't leave us now." Cassie's screams echoed through the house as she tried to rally her father. "Mama, do something, please. Please, Mama, don't let my daddy leave me again, Mama."

Cassie's shrilling cries sent shockwaves through Thomas' head before his eyes glazed over. Jenny held her daughter to her chest and rocked her as she tried to comfort her.

"No, Mama," she said, pulling away from Jenny, "you *don't* understand. My daddy can't die now. He can't!"

Thomas began to gasp for deep breaths and grimaced in pain before he took one last heave and passed away.

"Oh God," Jenny cried, bending over as though the wind had been knocked out of her. "Oh God, no, this can't be happening. This is too much for me to bear."

Her tears flowed uncontrollably. Surely this was a nightmare that would soon end. Jenny tried to catch her breath as waves of nausea rolled her stomach. She was sure that she had these terrible dreams before. Jenny just wanted to wake up and hear Thomas tell her it was just a bad dream. But the pain was too real, and the sight of her daughter's hysteria quickly heightened her fears.

Jenny leaned over, tapping Thomas gently on the face and then shaking him, hoping to somehow rouse him. Her stomach was sick, and her head throbbing. She could hear it pulsating louder than her voice. "Thomas, Thomas... oh Thomas, please don't leave me, Thomas. Dear Jesus," she cried, "help me, help Thomas."

Barely able to catch her breath Jenny was sure it was her life that was over. She would call a different doctor. Surely someone could help. How could she possibly live without the only human being that truly loved her? Life without Thomas was not a life. The pain was unimaginable. How could she go on? What would be the point?

Bloneva soon returned from taking T. J. on his afternoon stroll. Cassie ran down the driveway to find her when she realized her daddy was dead.

"You said your God would listen to me," she shouted angrily at Bloneva. "You promised that He would take care of my daddy. You lied to me, and I hate you. I hate all of you. I want my daddy; don't you know that I need my daddy?"

Bloneva reached out to embrace Cassie, but she managed to evade her housekeeper's grasp. She grabbed T.J. from the stroller and ran inside to Thomas' room. The atmosphere was heavy, and the scent of his medications stronger than she had previously noticed. Even though the ceiling fan blew fresh gusts of wind, the room felt as though the oxygen had been dragged out and stored elsewhere.

Jenny sat beside Thomas on the bed, stroking his hair and talking to him. Her energy had waned from crying. She wouldn't let herself believe Thomas was dead.

"You've got to wake up, Thomas. I know you're tired, love...but we'll get through this together," she whispered. "I need you, Darling. You can't leave me now." Bloneva looked at Thomas and checked for his pulse. He was dead. His body had already started to stiffen.

"Dear Lord," she cried out, "you mean to say Mr. Thomas is truly gone. Oh, Ms. Jenny, I'm so sorry. I'm so sorry, Ms. Jenny, Mr. Thomas was a good man."

"It's okay, Bloneva. I think he's just tired. He's sleeping. You know he's been sleeping a lot lately."

Bloneva shook her head as tears streamed down her face. "No, no, Ms. Jenny, don't do that to yourself. Mr. Thomas is gone. He fought hard, Ma'am, but now he's free from all that pain. We gonna miss him, that's for sure."

Jenny knew Bloneva was right about the pain being over, but her heart was so heavy, and the room seemed to reel around her she could only think of her loss. She flopped on the chair next to her husband's bedside and wept uncontrollably once again. Her tears turned to deep moans from the pit of her stomach.

"It's not fair. We only just got him back. How could this happen to me? Oh, Thomas, please, Thomas, Darling, please don't leave me!"

"There, there, Ms. Jenny," Bloneva comforted her, "it's alright to cry—let it all out. You need to get it all out so that you can tend to your little ones."

"The little ones?" Jenny held her head up. She had forgotten that Cassie was beside her a moment ago. She scanned the room for her little girl as she wiped the tears from her face. How could she forget her daughter? Jenny raced out of the room looking for Cassie, doubly heartbroken that she had ignored her daughter.

~Chapter Forty-five~

Two years had passed since Thomas' death. Though Jenny was trying very hard to adjust to life without him, it was an even greater ordeal for Cassie, who was becoming a rebellious juvenile. For two years, Jenny mourned, and for two years, Bloneva cautioned her about Cassie's behavior.

"She's grieving," Jenny explained, "she'll get over it. We just have to be there for her, that's all."

Cassie didn't quite see it that way. She didn't want anyone to be there for her. If she couldn't have her daddy, she didn't want anybody. In fact, she wanted so much to be dead like him than to live another day without him. Cassie's grades dropped in school. Her teachers were concerned for her, as she had adopted a habit of missing classes whenever she felt a notion to. Her choice of friends seemed less than desirable, and soon, at age twelve and a half, Cassie's life was spiraling downhill. It seemed that the more Jenny tried to communicate with her daughter, the more unapproachable Cassie became.

Before long Jenny's finances were dwindling. She would have to give up the home on Ford Hill. The thought of having to give up the one thing that held so many memories for them as a family was a hard decision for Jenny to make. She knew she had to break the news to Cassie, but she wasn't sure how she would receive it.

"Cassie, I need to talk to you a moment," Jenny called to her daughter.

"I'm busy, Mama," she mumbled as she swished past her mother impudently. Jenny grabbed her daughter by the arm and pulled her close.

"What didn't you understand, Cassandra?" she told her crisply, "I said I would like to talk with you, and I do mean now."

Jenny was fed up with her daughter's behavior. In her day, children were thrashed for that kind of insolence. Cassie was surprised at her mother's response. Jenny had allowed Cassie to walk over her and have her own way since her dad had passed away, and now she had surprisingly become more spirited.

"That's better," Jenny said to her daughter as she noted the shock on her face. Jenny sat down on the sofa in the living room and waited for Cassie to do the same before speaking.

"Our finances have been a little tight recently. The savings your dad and I had is dwindling very quickly...the long and short of it is we have to make a few adjustments in our lifestyle." Jenny paused, wondering if any of what she had said registered to her daughter, who had a blank look on her face.

"This house has become too difficult to manage without an income. I believe it will only be temporary until I get myself a job, but we'll be okay." Cassie seemed lost for words or did not care one way or the other what her mother said. "I had to let Bloneva go today and we must begin looking into a new home immediately.

"Is that it, Mother?" Cassie asked crisply, attempting to dismiss the conversation.

"Yes, Cassie, for now anyway. But let me also inform you that your attitude will also be undergoing some major adjustments."

Jenny got up to attend to T. J., who had just awakened from his nap as Cassie sauntered off. Fortunately, her son was too young to understand what had been going on for the past two years. Jenny embraced T.J. tightly before checking his diaper.

~Chapter Forty-six~

"I believe this will suit me** well, Sir." Jenny turned to Mr. Parker as he completed her tour of the quaint cottage bordering his lovely home.

It was evident that the Parkers had taken much pride in their property, and Jenny felt that it was only a matter of time before he had taken care of the repairs the cottage needed.

"Well, Mrs. Ford, me and the wife were sorry to hear of your late husband's ordeal. It must have been a great loss for you and the children."

Jenny thought it was kind of Mr. Parker to say so. "Yes, Sir, it was a great loss." Mr. Parker put his hands in his pocket and winked at Jenny coyly.

"A fine looking woman like you won't have any problem finding another catch like your white fella, though. You know what they say," Mr. Parker continued, completely oblivious to the look of absolute disgust on Jenny's face. "You know they say the darker the berry, the sweeter the juice!"

Jenny was not amused. "Mr. Parker, please hear me well because I hope I will not have to repeat myself. For the record, I am interested in renting your cottage. I am not interested in your unpalatable comments. In fact, if I do decide to live here, I will prefer it if you would respect our privacy. I am interested in your cottage, Mr. Parker, nothing more!"

Jenny was never one to mince her words, especially with folks who made it their business to interfere in her private affairs.

"Now, now, sweet girl, you don't have to get all fiery with me. I'm only trying to be neighborly."

Well, neighborly was not what Jenny had in mind. This man had already shown his colors, and she was not interested in any of them.

"Mr. Parker, it's Mrs. Ford. Now, if you'd kindly fill me in on your rental requirements, I will see that they are satisfied."

Taken aback by Jenny's remarks, Mr. Parker stuttered for a moment. If he weren't in such desperate need of money, he would have turned her away.

"It's the usual, first, last, and security deposit. You pay for your own water, gas, electricity, and telephone. And since you have taken it upon yourself to be so blunt, I feel it equally necessary to inform you that rent is due on the first of every month and not a day later. Furthermore, me and the wife, well, we don't like noise, so make sure y'all keep quiet up in here." Jenny walked towards her car and looked back at Mr. Parker.

"I'll expect those repairs to be made as you promised. I'll have your money to you in the morning."

Dealing with Mr. Parker was like pulling teeth. If it wasn't in writing, his word changed with every fleeting fancy. Three weeks later, Jenny and her family moved into the Parker cottage an hour's drive southwest of Ford Hill. Her heart was heavy as she transported the last of her personal belongings. Fortunately, she had a sale for the house, and the new owners were eager to move in. They were more than delighted to hire Bloneva at Jenny's suggestion.

"Ms. Jenny, it was awfully nice of you to put in a good word for me with Mrs. Harrison. They look like mighty fine people, and I could use the job right now."

"I'm so sorry I can't take you along with me, Bloneva. We are going to miss you a whole lot."

The drive to Jenny's new home was too much of an ordeal for Bloneva's car to make. She figured the mileage covered in one day would be equal to a week's worth of driving in the village, even if she decided to suggest a pay cut, something she could ill afford. Besides which, Jenny felt that Cassie was old enough to handle a few more household chores. Between the two of them, the cottage could be kept orderly.

So grateful for Jenny's kindness to her and the villagers, Bloneva insisted on coming to the cottage to help Jenny clean up. She had heard about Mr. Parker and knew well that he would not have the place fit to move in. The cottage had been in a state of disrepair for years and would never be considered worthy of his money to outfit the building or the gardens like his home, which was a mere stone's throw away.

"You all just need to go now and find something to busy yourself with while I give this old place a good scouring."

Bloneva knew that the little place was way below her former employer's standard. She had discussed it with Ike also, who wanted to do all he could to help his aunt. He had offered to move out of her house in the village so that she and her kids could move in, but Jenny would not consider it. There were far too many memories latched to her childhood home, and pushing Ike out would be completely insensitive. She figured it best to move away from the village entirely.

As soon as Bloneva could convince Jenny to leave the cottage and take a break, Ike showed up with a few of his friends and some supplies. Together they worked feverishly cleaning and painting the inside of the cottage. By the time Bloneva finished placing the area rug on the floor in the living room, the house was transformed and ready for its new residents to make it their home.

Ike had already decided that he would return the following day to cheer up the yard somewhat. At least little T.J. would have an area to play outdoors and wouldn't be confined to the inside because of the shrubbery overgrowth. He knew he had to make himself more available for his aunt, as Mr. Parker was not interested in repairing or maintaining the property himself.

The yellow Volkswagen remained parked in front of her new home when Jenny returned that evening. Quite surprised Bloneva was still there, Jenny handed a few of her packages to Cassie as they walked to the front door. It was getting late, and Bloneva's family would be concerned if they knew she would be driving such a distance by herself on the unlit road. Bloneva quickly opened the door with a huge grin plastered on her face.

"Ta-da!" she sang out as Jenny walked through the door. Jenny was utterly amazed at how the cottage had been transformed.

"Bloneva, what have you done?"

Bloneva rubbed her hands together excitedly, "do you like it, Ms. Jenny?" she quizzed.

"You are a dear, Bloneva. I love it. It almost reminds me of home," she replied.

"Well, that's exactly what Ike said too!"

Jenny swung around to Bloneva. "Ike was here? I didn't know he was coming by," she stated, a bit surprised.

Bloneva winked at Jenny. "We couldn't tell you, Ma'am, 'cause we knew you'd say no."

Cassie walked into her bedroom. It was certainly not as drab as she left it. Not that she had any intention of spending much time there anyway.

"Recognize the paint, Ma'am? We got it from the tool shed. This is the leftover paint from when you had Ike freshen up your walls a short time back." Jenny walked around the cottage. Bloneva and Ike had done an incredible job.

The kitchen looked like food could now be prepared and eaten in it. Bloneva had spent most of her time in the kitchen and the single bathroom scouring the cabinets until they looked almost brand new. She had only wished that she were able to work some kind of miracle on the tub. Although it was soaked in bleach for most of the day, the acid stains would not budge. Ike thought perhaps he could paint it another day. In the meantime, a rubber mat and a quick shower would have to do.

"I am so moved, Bloneva—this is the greatest gift you could have ever given me." Bloneva collected her belongings along with the last bag of garbage.

"Ms. Jenny, I hope you won't be too scarce. I would really like to see the children on occasion if it's alright with you."

Jenny took the bag from Bloneva while discreetly slipping some money into her hand. Bloneva was alarmed. She had no intention of accepting payment for what she had done.

"Oh no, Ms. Jenny, I couldn't possibly take this. You buy something nice for the children with this for me." Bloneva walked to the door and she smiled up at their handiwork once again. "Tell the children so long for me, Ma'am. I'm not so good with goodbyes myself," her eyes watered slightly as she spoke.

~Chapter Forty-seven~

"**If Eric says you can make a good** go at modeling again, Aunt Jen, why not go for it?" Ike encouraged his aunt. "It would probably do you just as much good as the kids to get away and have a change of environment for a while."

The thought had occurred to Jenny many times, especially after having to deal with Cassie's poor choice of friends. The truth of the matter was she did enjoy modeling, and though she would only make a fraction of what she had made initially, her income would be more than ideal to live comfortably.

It was difficult raising the children without a man in the home. When he was able, and when he thought it necessary, Ike made a point of visiting his aunt to check on her and the kids. Both he and Jenny thought Cassie would have stabilized by now. In a few weeks she would be thirteen and had gotten herself into far too many close scrapes with unsavory company.

Jenny thought about moving to London to look into reviving her fledgling modeling career. She knew it was a long shot, but according to Eric, she could still make a good living from modeling if she was willing to work at it.

"I believe you're right to give it a try, Aunt Jenny," Ike agreed. "It just might be the fresh start you need as a family to get on a better footing. Maybe it would help to bond you and Cassie together being away from here."

Ike had seen the strain. It was also beginning to affect little Thomas.

"Anyway, you tell me what you need, Aunt Jen, and consider it done."

Jenny tapped her nephew on his fingers. "Ike, what would I have done without you all these years?"

Ike shrugged his shoulders, "Well since you put it that way, I guess it wouldn't have been a whole lot." Jenny laughed. Even at such a dark place in her life, Ike still managed to put a smile on her face.

Though he did not wish to burden his aunt unnecessarily, Ike was concerned about Cassie's reputation with the boys in the village. Without sounding too pushy, he continued to encourage Jenny about his young cousin attending an all-girls boarding school. She needed to steer clear from the boys for a while.

Once Jenny had initiated her inquiry, packages began to flood the little cottage from schools all around the London area. There was one that stood out from them all. It was a well-established school, having enrollments from all over the world, including Kenya, Jordan, Taiwan, and the Caribbean.

Initially, Cassie was not interested in leaving the island or going to an all-girls school. Ike knew that it was a tough decision for Jenny to make, but he stood by her completely and reaffirmed the move with Cassie when she had called him to complain of the prison camp her mother was planning on sending her.

"I'll read up on a few of the schools, Ike," she informed him cautiously, "but I'm not making any promises."

In time, Cassie became quite enthralled with the idea of boarding school. It was one way of getting away from her mother for a while and another way of meeting up with some really cool girls who were daughters of famous models and even royalty. The more she read about Braebury College, she became increasingly inclined to enroll there.

Although the school was considered one of the smallest in the country, it boasted successes in academics, sports, dance, and drama. Many of Braebury's graduates achieved success in theater and dance, occasionally visiting their alma mater to inspire other young hopefuls.

So it was decided, Braebury College was the high school of choice. Jenny was delighted that Cassie had finally come around. Notwithstanding her decision to enroll her daughter, regardless of her final thoughts.

The school on the outskirts of London insisted on Jenny's enrolling her daughter as a weekly boarder, for the first year at least. From there, if she wanted to be a day student, she would have already settled into their system without outside interference. It was not an option, Cassie was informed. The school would assist in bringing her grades up if she did her part. An added bonus to Jenny was the school's strict dress code. Uniforms were worn every day of the week. This would eliminate Cassie's new urge to wear the latest unbecoming clothing that was the rage of the day.

~Chapter Forty-eight~

The trip to London was a long, sobering one. Cassie pressed her face against the window of the aircraft. She felt scared and alone. Hot tears flowed down her cheeks. It was the first time she had cried since her father passed away. At age thirteen, Cassie felt like her world was upside down. She had spent so much of her time pushing her mother away from her they were almost complete strangers. Jenny reached over to her daughter and stroked her hair.

"I love you, Cass. I want you to know that." Cassie clenched her eyes tighter. How could her mother love her after all the hateful things she intentionally said and done to push her away. Jenny released her seatbelt and moved closer to Cassie. Thomas was already sleeping and quite content to rest across his mother's lap.

"Sweetheart," Jenny pulled her daughter to her, "it's been rough for both of us. We've said some harsh things in the past, but I want you to know that there is nothing you can say or do to erase the love I have for you."

The events of the past few years passed through Cassie's mind. She remembered the day she openly rebelled against her mother and decided to live life her way. It seemed like her ugly behavior had poured out of the woodwork and coated her like fresh mud every day. Cassie remembered vividly the people that sought her out to aid her in self-ruination. Folks she had never paid attention to before or, in some cases, never met before befriended her, teaching her the tricks of rebellion. They openly scoffed at her when she told them of her father's death and her desire to just curl up and die to hasten her seeing him in heaven.

Her newly found comrades were quick to inform her that her father's new address was not heaven. Quite the contrary, they insisted, "He's in hell!" Cassie was considerably shaken at the time. Bloneva had spoken to her quite extensively about heaven but omitted any mention of hell. Her newfound friends were quite convincing. If she loved her father so much, and if he was as nice a person as Cassie said, then God was a liar, and she was better off in hell with her father.

"At least," they rationalized, "you would be with him forever."

Cassie thought so too. At least until Bloneva told her that those people were messengers from the pit of the devil himself. She had never seen her old faithful housekeeper so upset.

"If I thought it would do you some good, Child," Bloneva warned her, "I'd lay you across my lap and smack some sense into you." Bloneva was livid. "Your daddy's in heaven with Jesus, young lady! I heard him pray and ask Jesus to forgive him of his sins. Why do you think for the last seven weeks he was here with us? He used to call you to read his Bible to him too."

It was all coming back to Cassie now. She had been so thick-skulled and bitter she pushed everybody away from her. She couldn't see what was plainly in front of her. Had she asked earlier, Bloneva would have told her quite willingly.

Cassie sighed. If she hadn't visited Bloneva for the last time before leaving for London, she would have never known the truth. How her mother could ever forgive her for the monster she had become was nothing short of miraculous. She did promise Bloneva that she would make a good effort at her new school.

Bloneva looked at Cassie with tears in her eyes, "I've been praying for you, chile. God knows I scorched up my old knees as I cried out to Him to bring my sweet girl back to us." Cassie remembered being swallowed up by Bloneva's big chubby arms. "Now, if you really want to see your daddy again, girl, you have to do what he did," Bloneva insisted as she comforted Cassie.

Cassie wept as Bloneva held her tightly. She wanted to see her daddy all right, but now she was beginning to realize that the God whom Bloneva served cared for her and was offering her even more than just seeing her dad again. Cassie hadn't told her mother of her and Bloneva's meeting. She couldn't explain it, but she felt lighter on the inside. She knew something had changed in her life. It was as though a big dark curtain were ripped from her eyes, permitting beautiful light to shine in. Cassie turned and clung to her mother. She knew that her mother loved her and her brother more than anything else.

"Mama, I'm so sorry. I know that I haven't been acting like myself lately." Jenny rocked her daughter quietly, allowing her to get what was bothering her off her chest. "I wanted you to feel the hurt I felt when Daddy died. I wanted to die too, Mama," she wept uncontrollably. "It hurt so much. I missed daddy, and I wanted to be with him. Then I started to get scared, Mama, because I would sometimes have to get his picture to remember his face."

Tears rolled down Jenny's face as she felt the pain in Cassie's voice. Her daughter and husband had a special relationship. Jenny marveled at how Thomas brought out the best in their daughter. She never knew that it was even possible for a father to love a daughter as Thomas did. Jenny's own experience with her father was quite the opposite. A few minutes later, a flight attendant passed with a box of tissue and two cups of water.

"I thought you two might need this," she said quietly as she rested the items on the tray in front of Jenny. Jenny thanked the young lady graciously as she handed the box to Cassie, whose eyes were red and puffed. The cabin lights were already dimmed, and most of the passengers had nodded off.

"I guess we look a sight, Cass," she grinned. Cassie wiped under her mom's eyes where her mascara had smeared.

"That's better now, Mama. By the time we reach London, our eyes won't be so puffy," Cassie giggled."

Fortunately for little Thomas, it was a late-night flight, which coincided wonderfully with his sleep schedule. The only problem was the time adjustments they would have to make for the first few days. Cassie and Jenny spoke for hours. It was like getting to know each other all over again.

"Mama, tell me how you and Daddy met. Did you love him as soon as you saw him?" Jenny smiled at her daughter and shook her head.

"Oh no, Cass, when I met your daddy I didn't even know what love was."

Cassie looked surprised. "But everybody in the village loves you. What do you mean you didn't know what love was?" Jenny realized that she had never really talked to Cassie about her childhood days. Her daughter was under the impression that she had lived a rosy life from her birth.

"Oh no, my darling, you see, I never knew my mother. She died just after she gave birth to me. I knew things would have been different if she had lived, but she didn't, and I still had to make the best out of my situation."

"What about your father, and Ike's mom and all your sisters and brother, didn't they love you?" Jenny thought for a while.

"If they did, I wasn't aware of it. My daddy and my old Aunt Bessie raised me after my mama had passed on. They blamed me for her death and considered me to be a burden. Daddy hardly spoke to me, and when he did, it wasn't pleasant at all. But I had something burning on the inside driving me to do better, to be better. I knew I wasn't born just for a slavish life. I read books. I begged my aunt to let me go to school. I knew I had to do something special with my life."

"So that's why you moved to the mainland?" Jenny nodded.

"Uh-huh, I didn't think there was anything worth staying home for. I was terribly unhappy." Cassie furrowed her eyebrows.

"How could you be so unhappy if Dad was there? Didn't you know him? I thought he lived in the village." Jenny smiled as she reflected on her first meeting with Thomas.

"Actually, I got my first job working for your daddy. He needed someone to look after his grandmother. I was the only person who was willing to do it. We became friends, and then I left to find a better life on the mainland. I didn't know that your dad cared about me until I came home several years later to visit my ailing father."

Cassie was enthralled with her mothers' childhood. Though she couldn't figure how her mom just didn't stay and marry her dad earlier instead of leaving the island.

"Like you say, Mama, 'that's water underneath the bridge' I suppose I should just be satisfied that you did finally marry Dad." Jenny and Cassie continued talking until their eyes could stay open no longer. When she glanced over at her daughter, she saw a measure of contentment on her face as never before.

"Thank you, Lord," she whispered as she closed her eyes for the remainder of the flight.

~Chapter Forty-nine~

I t was quite challenging to determine whether or not they liked London. Everything looked grey once they pierced through the blanket of clouds as they made their final approach to Heathrow Airport. Once in the airport, Cassie stayed close to her mom, who looked quite confident for an island girl in a big city. Everyone looked busy, not even caring to make eye contact with a fellow traveler. Cassie was careful not to complain but did note that very few people smiled or greeted them as they did on Maruba.

In fact, there was no resemblance of Maruba anywhere. The cars were tiny, and even though they drove on the left, the British cars were right-hand drives. Instead of the big cheery taxis, all local cabs were the same odd-shaped black vehicles. Their roads were really wide, which helped to accommodate the great number of cars, taxis, and cherry red double-decker buses.

It was cold and rainy, not what Cassie expected of the temperature as they approached summer. Although they were bundled up in their warm winter attire, most people were dressed in lightweight clothing—clothing that could be worn on the island on a cool evening.

The kids were hungry, and Jenny wanted nothing more than to get off of her feet after a nine-hour flight coupled with the long trek through the airport to collect their luggage. Although Eric could not meet them, he had a limousine sent to collect them and take them to their temporary residence—a modest bed and breakfast in Central London.

Eric was also kind enough to link Jenny up with a realtor who spent several hours showing Jenny several possible three-bedroom "flats," as he called them. For almost two weeks, Jenny and the children scoured the newspaper and beat the pavements hoping to find a place they could call home.

Just when they thought they could walk no more, they stumbled across a lovely three-bedroom apartment. The outside of the building was not appealing in the least—the standard red brick building looked pretty much like all the other buildings on the street. Jenny loved the inside immediately. The high ceilings and the fairly open plan made the flat seem larger. Both Jenny and Cassie liked the idea that it was pretty close to a park and virtually walking distance to a nearby gym and grocery store.

"I'll take it," Jenny told the landlord. "When will it be ready?"

"It's available now, Madam. Apart from paying the rent, all you need are your personal effects." Jenny took a copy of the lease with her to study overnight. It appeared to be straightforward enough. Several days later, after shopping for a few household items, the Ford's began to move into their new home.

One of Jenny's priorities was to take the children on a few tours to familiarize them with the city. Little Thomas wanted nothing more than to ride on the top level of the double-decker busses while Cassie wanted to visit Buckingham Palace and Madame Tussauds wax museum. She would have to see when and how to figure that into their already hectic schedule.

After they had settled in and found a pre-school for T.J. to enroll in, Jenny and Cassie went in search of Braebury College. Cassie was excited since it was her first time traveling on a train. Jenny calculated their journey from their new flat to the school to take just over an hour. Though the school was closed for the summer, they were given a tour of the facilities and shown the dormitory Cassie would more than likely be staying in. It was a pleasure meeting the staff. They were every bit as congenial and professional as their correspondence alluded. In three weeks, Cassie would be a student of Braebury.

By that time, T.J. would have gotten accustomed to his little school. For now, Jenny thought to let him spend several hours each day playing with other kids his age. Thomas loved it. Cassie was happy, and Eric was eager to set up Jenny's initial shoots. Jenny knew she had kept him at bay long enough and made arrangements to come for a few hours each week until Cassie was settled into school. It was important for Jenny not to have her children feel as though they had been abandoned at such a critical time in their lives.

For the first time since her husband's death, Jenny was beginning to feel like her life was coming together. Jenny missed Thomas more than she had dreamt possible. She knew she had to carry on with her life now. Thomas would have insisted upon it. Simply looking at the children brought floods of memories of Thomas. Her heart was warmed when little Thomas smiled. He looked so much like his dad when he did. As for Cassie, she bore a striking resemblance to her father in many ways.

Jenny's eyes welled with tears as she thought of her husband. He was a wonderful man—brave, loving, and kind. She was glad that he was finally free from his pain. She smiled to herself as the memory of Thomas proposing to her flashed through her mind. The almost eleven marvelous years of marriage were something she would always be grateful for. Plus the two lovely children he had given her. Jenny seriously doubted that any man could ever fill Thomas' shoes. For one to even try would be a complete waste of time.

~Chapter Fifty~

Thomas raced up the steps with his mother to their second-floor apartment. He was a bundle of energy and, as always, totally oblivious to what was going on around him. Thomas' world was bright, free, and happy. Most of the tenants in the building were young professionals of varied nationalities who lived very much to themselves. Quite unlike the environment Jenny and her children grew up in, where everyone knew each other.

Mr. and Mrs. Rodriguez, an elderly couple, lived down the hall from Jenny. They were thrilled to have warm neighbors such as the Ford's in the building and equally pleased to hear that Jenny was from the West Indies as they were. But most of all, they loved Thomas. Thomas made a special point to call their neighbor every time he saw them in the park. On days when it was a little too wet for him to go out, he stayed in, painting pictures for Mrs. Rodriguez.

As Jenny got closer to the elderly couple she realized that though they were incredibly independent, they did have some difficulty traveling in the cold weather. Without even a second thought or request, she would pick up a few items from the store and sometimes even prepare special meals for them. Thomas had adopted the Rodriguez couple as his new grandparents, much to their delight.

"Mrs. Rodriguez," Jenny called out to her neighbor as she knocked on the door.

It was awfully quiet, and she hadn't seen them in several days. That really wasn't unusual if she were on a special fashion shoot, but she wasn't, and her neighbors were especially quiet. After a little while, Mrs. Rodriguez came to the door. She looked worn out and a bit under the weather.

"Oh my, no wonder I haven't seen you, you poor dear. Why didn't you call to say that you weren't well?"

"Oh Jenny, we're so used to taking care of each other we didn't think to bother you," the old woman whispered, covering her throat with her hand as she spoke.

"Well, I'm more bothered that you didn't call me. Now back to bed, and I'll take care of you from here on in," Jenny assured the old lady.

Mr. Rodriguez was sleeping. The cold medication kept him sedated most of the time. The problem was Mrs. Rodriguez had worn herself out looking after the old man until she too became ill.

"What you need is a hot cup of tea and some chicken soup. I'm going to make you the best soup you've had in your life!" Mrs. Rodriguez was feeling better already, just having Jenny around.

"You sure are something special, girl. Gracias, Amorsita," she said, lapsing into her native language. Around the home, both Mr. and Mrs. Rodriguez communicated in Spanish, except when company was present.

Mrs. Rodriguez paused for a moment, "Jenny," she asked, "have you seen Tibbles? The poor cat must have gone looking for a new master. I don't think I've fed him for the whole week." Jenny helped the old lady back into her bed.

"I'll look around and set out a plate of food for him. Don't you worry about a thing. But first," she said, fluffing Mrs. Rodriguez' pillows, "I'm going to make you a nice hot cup of tea, then I'm going home to prepare the soup for you."

Mrs. Rodriguez reached over to her nightstand and picked up her keys. "Here, Child, you'll need these to get back in."

Jenny slipped the keys into her pocket and went into the kitchen to make the tea. Everything seemed so chaotic in the refrigerator that she made a mental note to come back another day to organize it for her neighbor. She pulled out the fruit tray in search of fresh lemon for the tea. A reddish-brown substance had dripped from the shelf above in the fruit compartment.

"Oh, dear," Jenny exclaimed at the sight of the mess.

She couldn't leave the refrigerator in such a disorderly state. Mrs. Rodriguez was so caught up with taking care of her husband she had overlooked whatever had been leaking below.

"I guess I'll have to clean this now," she muttered as she pulled the lemon out of the tray. "Just as soon as I brew this pot of tea."

Mixing her island favorite of lemon and honey tea, Jenny picked up two cups and saucers from the cupboard. "Here you are, Dear," she said to the old lady as she placed a fresh pot of tea on the nightstand. I brought an extra cup for Mr. Rodriguez just in case he gets up soon."

Fortunately, Thomas was taking his afternoon nap. He had a full day at school today and an equally full list of tales to tell. Jenny knew that if she worked swiftly, she could have the refrigerator cleaned and the soup well on its way before Thomas awoke. From the looks of the inside of the fridge, neither of the Rodriguez's had much of an appetite for food.

Virtually everything that was not bottled had to be thrown out, including the source of the reddish brown fluid. Jenny opened the box gingerly, not knowing what to expect of its contents. Her eyes fluttered before screaming and dropping the box on the kitchen floor. The oozing liquid and the pungent smell sent her reeling to the counter. Mr. Rodriguez came shuffling out of the bedroom, concerned about the noise he had just heard. Seconds later, Mrs. Rodriguez was behind him.

"What on earth is the matter, Jenny? Are you alright?" he asked, concerned for her well-being.

"What is it, Dear?" his wife quizzed. Jenny tried to calm herself as she patted her chest, hoping to slow down her racing heartbeat. She turned away from the refrigerator and pointed to the box on the floor.

"Mrs. Rodriguez," she said, her mouth barely able to form the words. "I think I've just found Tibbles!" Mr. Rodriguez leaned over the counter and laughed hysterically, both his wife and Jenny not understanding what quite humored him.

"Mavis, que te pasa? I thought you put that old thing in storage." Mrs. Rodriguez held her mouth as though she had forgotten a very important task.

"No se, mi amor. You know, Honey, I just plain forgot when you got sick." Jenny looked back and forth to the couple, not understanding what they were talking about or why they were so calm. Seeing the shock still registered on her face, Mr. Rodriguez shuffled around the mess on the floor and picked up the box.

"Don't be afraid, Jenny," he cautioned. "This little fluffy thing in here is not Tibbles. It's my wife's fox stole." I bought it for her a couple years ago. I thought I would give her a piece of fur that would remind me of how foxy she used to look!

Mrs. Rodriguez laughed at her husband, who was always kidding her. "Otis, tell the truth. You bought it because you couldn't afford to buy the whole fur coat."

Mr. Rodriguez shook his head, smiling. "No, I bought it because it was on sale!"

Jenny still wasn't convinced. "Well, what about the blood and that odor?"

Mrs. Rodriguez grimaced, "I felt so weak yesterday when I was pouring Otis some beetroot juice that I knocked over the carton in the fridge. It slipped my mind after that. Ordinarily, I would have cleaned it up right away."

Mr. Rodriguez put his arm around his wife's shoulder. She was always so busy looking after him that she had forgotten about her stole. They had kept it in the refrigerator for safekeeping.

"You girls carry on smartly. I'll clean up this mess."

"Oh no, you two have been on your feet too long as it is. Now I would appreciate it if you would go back to bed and let me complete this task." Jenny answered firmly. She took the stole out and put it on a clean surface.

"I'll drop it by the cleaners tomorrow," she promised her neighbors. "Now please go back to bed. I didn't mean to alarm you.

"Otis, this is the most energy I've seen you have all week," his wife teased. "You bolted out here like lightning. I think you've been playing on my sympathy for service." Mr. Rodriguez hugged his wife and winked at Jenny while walking her back to their bedroom.

"Mavis, it was only because of your loving care that I was able to get up like that. You sure know how to love hard. It gives me such strength, Amorcita."

Jenny smiled as the two of them hobbled back to their room together. It would only take a few minutes to wipe down the fridge, as practically everything else had to be thrown away. Then she would go home to make the soup.

~Chapter Fifty-one~

Several **days later, Jenny** was still catering to the Rodriguez's needs. She was happy to be available for them. They both were getting stronger and loved the attention Jenny was pouring on them. She was fast becoming the daughter they had always wanted and never had.

"If I wasn't so old, I'd adopt you and call you mine," Mrs. Rodriguez told her one day.

"That's the nicest thing anyone's said to me all day, Mrs. Rodriguez. Thank you."

"Why adopt her, Mavis?" Mr. Rodriguez chimed in. His strength had quickly expressed itself in his mouth just as Mrs. Rodriguez had predicted. "Why don't you just trade her in for one of our sons? Or just make it an even switch—how about the two of them?"

Mrs. Rodriguez chuckled. Otis was always threatening to trade in their children for more reliable models. The truth was he doted on both of them. He was proud of his two boys—he only wished he could see more of them.

"Now, Otis, you know that they have their own lives now. Nicky can't come as often since his job transferred him to Milan, and Anton says he's moving back to London as soon as his divorce has been finalized."

Jenny was used to the two old folks making sport with each other, but she had often wondered why they didn't have someone looking after them.

Anton Rodriguez was a smooth dark skinned handsome young man with straight black hair. He was born and raised in the Dominican Republic, having migrated to London with his parents when his younger brother Nicky was born. Anton and his wife Emily had a turbulent marriage. As a last-ditch effort to save their relationship, Anton agreed to relocate to his wife's home in Mexico. Despite his efforts, the marriage failed, and an embittered custody feud for their three children followed.

"Don't you listen to Otis, dear. Our boys are good decent people, and we're proud of them both." Mrs. Rodriguez pulled out a little photo album from the coffee table. "This is our Nicky, Jenny. He's a banker."

Jenny chuckled to herself. All of Mrs. Rodriguez's photos were of her children in their early teenage years. Seeing a picture of a fourteen-year-old boy and placing him in a banker's chair was quite humorous. Mr. Rodriguez leaned over to Jenny and gave her a nudge.

"What Mavis is trying to say is that Nicky is single, and he's got no one but us to spend his money on." Jenny laughed. She had never seen Mr. Rodriguez so mischievous before.

"But if you think he's too young for you, Anton is a fine boy too. He's had his share of problems with Emily, but he'll be alright." Mr. Rodriguez turned to his wife and winked, "As a matter of fact, Mavis, I think Jenny is just what the doctor ordered for our boy."

Mrs. Rodriguez tapped her husband playfully on his knee, "Otis, don't you go scaring Jenny off now. That wouldn't be nice at all."

Jenny looked at Anton's photograph. He looked pensive, as though he was carrying the world on his shoulders despite his youthfulness. Jenny smiled at the elderly couple; she actually enjoyed their company. Though she hastened to add for the record that she was not interested in dating anyone at this time, and that included their handsome sons. Her hands were completely full with Cassie and Thomas. Mr. Rodriguez nodded his head.

It was true, her hands were full, and Jenny was a great mother. Her kids were quite fortunate to have her for a mom, but that didn't stop him from thinking of ways to get her hitched up with his Anton. He could use some joy in his life. Anton was just a few years older than Jenny yet acted like a stiff old English gentleman. Mr. Rodriguez felt that if his son met Jenny, he might just decide to embrace life before it was too late.

"Otis, I know what you're thinking. You'd better let well enough alone!" she warned her husband. "Remember, it was you who matched Anton up with Emily in the first place."

"There you go Mavis, digging up old dry bones. Woman, you need to go and work in a graveyard!" he puffed. "Well, since you brought it up, let me tell you something," he paused, turning to his wife. "If Emily hadn't let her husband's money go to her head, they would still be married today. One day she was a loving wife, the next, a social butterfly who listened to her idle friends! That would never work with Anton. He is a hard-working family man." Mrs. Rodriguez sat quietly, hoping her husband would drop the subject.

"Thomas and I are going to be away for about a week. Cassie has a mid-term break," Jenny informed her neighbors, attempting to change the heated subject. "We decided to take the train into North Wales. I've heard so much of Colwyn Bay that we decided it would be a good time to go for a visit together."

"Do you know anyone in the area, Dear?" Mrs. Rodriguez inquired.

"Why yes, one of Cassie's dorm-mates is from Colwyn Bay, and I've been in touch with her mom for a little while. We'll be in good hands, I'm sure. In fact, we'll be staying at a hotel near their house. I'll leave the contact information for you. It's called Rhos Abbey Hotel."

"Good girl, Jenny. Take in as much of the country as you can. Be sure to take the children to see the castles if you have time. Though you may have a full schedule just visiting the Colwyn Bay area," Mr. Rodriguez advised.

Mrs. Rodriguez was grateful for Jenny's kindness in changing the conversation. "What a lovely idea, Jenny. Well, give Cassie our love. I hope we'll get to see her before she goes back though."

Jenny hugged the old lady as she made her way to the door. "We'll make it a point to come and see you. Thomas has told her that he has a grandpa and nana."

Mr. Rodriguez cleared his throat, "That little boy has good sense... I say no more," he said, picking up the newspaper from the table beside him to read.

~Chapter Fifty-two~

Thomas **bolted up the stairs to** their apartment, screeching as he went. His mother ran behind him.

"I'm going to win this time, Thomas," she teased playfully, mincing her steps behind her five-year-old. Thomas turned excitedly, darting into a tall stranger before toppling to the floor.

"Oopsie," he said apologetically before racing to their door. Within seconds Jenny had followed in her son's footsteps, bumping into the same gentleman. Their corridor was generally empty during this time of day.

"Oh, I'm sorry, I didn't expect anyone to be here."

The gentleman extended his hand to Jenny and helped her up from the floor.

"I guess not," he stated matter-of-factly. "It's no bother. Actually, it was quite refreshing to see your son so happy."

Jenny waved at Thomas, who was tickled pink that he had won again. The stranger's face seemed a little familiar, but she wasn't sure. Jenny smiled nervously at the handsome gentleman and darted towards Thomas, scooping her giggling child up in her arms.

He turned to watch them as they went into their home. Jenny wondered why her heart was racing as she thought of the man. She had no idea who he was, but he certainly had a strange effect on her. As she pulled back her drapes to let the light in, Jenny glimpsed him at the roadside flagging down a cab. She wondered who he could be. He had such a commanding presence about him, and he was obviously quite wealthy too, by the looks of his clothing. The unit on the end of her floor was vacant, but she wasn't aware that anyone had moved in.

"Okay, Thomas, go and wash your hands and come to the table, love. I have a special treat for you today."

Thomas loved treats, and his newest favorite was a dish Mrs. Rodriguez would prepare for him from time to time.

"I know what it is, Mama," he said with a big grin on his face and ran to the bathroom down the hallway to wash up. "It's bangers and beans, right?"

"How did you get so smart, little fella? Its bangers and beans on toast."

Jenny could hear her son's yay's from the kitchen. Though life on the island was much simpler than in London, Jenny found their easy dishes a welcome after a long day at work.

Several days after their first encounter, Jenny and Thomas met the stranger coming down the stairs once again.

"I see you haven't lost any of that energy, young man, have you?"

Thomas smiled and shook his head as he continued to race up the stairs. Jenny and the stranger exchanged pleasantries and continued in the opposite direction.

Before Jenny could make it to her door, Thomas was already banging on their neighbor's door.

"Nana," he cried out, "Nana, it's me. I'm home." Mr. Rodriguez opened the door slowly and scooped Thomas up in his arms.

"Well, how are you today, Champ?" he asked the little boy. "Did you see any pretty girls in school today, or have they all left town?"

Thomas shrugged his shoulders, "I don't know. They all kinda look the same to me, Grampa."

Mr. Rodriguez ruffled the little boy's hair and kissed him on his cheek, "It won't always be that way son, trust me."

Jenny leaned against the door, her arms folded as she listened to her son's conversation.

"That's right, Thomas, they do all look alike, huh? When you've finished school and gotten a good job, then they could start developing features."

Mr. Rodriguez leaned over to Jenny and whispered in her ear. "Spoilsport, don't be a party pooper." Just as they were leaving, Mr. Rodriguez called out to Jenny,

"Oh, by the way, Sweetheart, it's the wife's birthday tomorrow. We'd be delighted if you would come over for some cake at about six o'clock."

Jenny blew the old man a kiss, "We wouldn't miss it for the world."

~Chapter Fifty-three~

T he tall dark stranger stood at the Rodriguez' door as Jenny and Thomas were about to walk over to the birthday celebration.

"So we meet again," his smooth deep voice jolting her from her thoughts, "I guess we should introduce ourselves. I'm Anton Rodriguez." Anton stretched his hand towards Jenny.

"It's a pleasure to meet you. I'm Jenny Ford, and this is my son Thomas."

Anton bent down to shake Thomas' hand.

"I'm glad to meet you, Thomas. I believe I've heard your name around these parts before. Oh yes, so you must be my parents' guardian angel." Anton got up and rang his parent's doorbell. "You must forgive my not recognizing your name."

Thomas rapped on the door and shouted, "Grampa, it's me Thomas." The door swung open, and Thomas dashed inside to see the birthday cake.

"I see you've met my son, Jenny." Mr. Rodriguez remarked, winking at Jenny as she stepped inside.

"That I have, Sir." Jenny followed her son to the sofa. "Where's the birthday girl?"

Mr. Rodriguez cleared his throat. "Oh, she just called. She's running a little late at the beauty parlor. As a matter of fact, I'm going to make a quick dash over there now to collect her."

Jenny placed her bag and the two gifts on the table, which she and Thomas brought over.

"Dad, there's no need for that. I'll go and collect her. You entertain your guest," Anton offered.

"Actually, Son, I was hoping that you would stay for me while I fetched your mom—if you don't mind."

Anton shrugged his shoulders, his dad seemed bent on going. Thomas had already gotten himself comfortable. His shoes were off, and his pullover lay in a mound next to him. It wasn't long before he had occupied himself with the toys that were kept in the corner of the room for his visits. Mr. Rodriguez quickly slipped out of the apartment before there was further ado.

"May I offer you a drink, Jenny?" Anton seemed almost as uncomfortable as Jenny felt.

"Actually, not right now, thanks, perhaps a little later."

After a little while, Jenny realized that they were set up. Their host should have been back some time ago. This was a typical set-up by Mr. Rodriguez. How he got his wife to be a part of his scheme was another thing. Anton figured it out also but attempted to be gracious.

"I think my folks are trying their hand at match-making Jenny. I'm sorry you had to go through this."

Jenny smiled at Anton, "I'm quite used to them. They mean well. They just think I need to have a man in my life again."

Anton reclined casually on his chair. He was so unassuming, though his good looks and fragrance were somewhat unnerving. In Jenny's line of work, it was not uncommon for her to meet extremely gorgeous men, but they knew it, and for the most part, that was the sum total of their entire being.

"Don't you?"

"Don't I what?" Jenny answered curtly.

"Don't you need a man in your life?"

Jenny sat back and glanced at her son. "No, Anton, I don't. I'm quite happy just as I am."

"Good for you," he answered, somewhat relieved that he didn't have to shake off another admirer. "Well, since that's out of the way, we can be friends."

Jenny was tempted to also inform him that she was not looking for friends either. Instead, she decided to hold her tongue.

"What is it that you do, Jenny, other than expend boundless energy with your son?"

"Oh, I'm in the arts." Jenny figured that was a safe answer. It had diverted the attention of many men in the past. That and the fact that she still wore her wedding ring when she wasn't working.

Anton, however, was unrelenting.

"What form?" Jenny picked a magazine casually and slapped it shut quickly when she saw a photograph of herself in it. "I guess you can say photographic."

Anton picked up the magazine.

"What is it that you do, Anton?" Jenny asked, hoping to have the conversation turned away from her.

"I dabble in sales and marketing. Doesn't sound very interesting, does it?"

"Actually, quite the contrary. I would love to hear more about it." Anton looked at the page in front of him and then back at Jenny. He tossed the magazine to the side and laughed.

"Let's call a truce, Jenny. Neither of us is interested in being set up. So let's come clean." Jenny looked surprised at Anton's remarks.

"You're a fashion model and a very beautiful one at that. I should have recognized you the moment I saw you."

Anton picked up the magazine from the floor. Though he was involved in the management side of his business and not so much the talent he recogninzed the label. His face brightened as he smiled.

"My company represents the line of clothing you're modeling. We've been marketing their products for the past several years."

Thomas was becoming a little restless. He had eaten virtually every treat Mr. Rodriguez left on the table. Thomas nestled on his mom's lap and fell asleep.

The phone rang. It was Mrs. Rodriguez, she apologized for their delay and reassured her son that they would be in shortly. Anton was enjoying Jenny's company immensely and was thankful of their time alone, though he dare not convey his thoughts. Quite unlike many women he had come in contact with recently, Anton found her refreshing, intelligent, and independent.

Jenny looked at her watch. It was getting late, and she had an early shoot in the morning.

"I'm afraid I must leave now. I have a full day ahead of me tomorrow." Anton stood up as Jenny gathered their belongings. It was a pleasure meeting you, Anton. I'm sorry your parents didn't make it back sooner." Anton nodded politely as he scooped Thomas up into his arms.

"I'll carry him, Jenny. Your hands are full, and there's no sense in waking the lad."

Jenny smiled, her hands were truly full, and if she had to wake her son, it would be quite trying putting him to bed once again.

"Thank you, I'll take you up on that offer." On her way out, Jenny quickly arranged the empty plates and glasses on the counter before securing the door behind Anton.

As Jenny pushed open her door, Anton carried her son down the hallway to the bedrooms.

"No, the second door on the right," she called behind him, not wanting him to linger in her bedroom.

Anton raised his eyebrows and smiled at Jenny. He was amused by her modesty. Jenny quickly shut the door behind him as he stepped out of her bedroom. Jenny's room was welcoming and filled with her warm, inviting fragrance.

Anton leaned over Thomas' bed as he pulled his comforter over his shoulder. His heart was heavy for a split second as he reflected on how each night he put his three sons to bed. Jenny watched his countenance change. It pulled at her heart.

"Can I interest you in a cup of hot chocolate, Anton?" she offered.

"I don't wish to impose, thank you anyway." He turned and looked at Thomas again before walking out of the room. "I was just remembering the times I put my boys to bed. I miss them very much," he confided.

"How old are your boys?" Jenny asked preparing the chocolate for the two of them.

"Carlos is eleven, Manuelo is nine, and Ricky is six. They are the greatest bunch of kids a man could ask for."

Jenny continued to listen as Anton told her colorful stories of his children's antics. Jenny laughed until her side hurt.

"They sound wonderful, Anton, I hope I can meet them someday."

~Chapter Fifty-four~

"**Hi, Mama,**" Cassie's voice rang through the phone. "I was wondering if I could bring a friend home with me this weekend. It's a new girl, she's quite nice, but she has no family over here."

This wasn't the first time Cassie had brought friends home for the weekend, and they all seemed like decent girls, which Jenny considered a total blessing.

"Sure, Sweetheart, you know the rules though, I must hear from the school personally before she can come out."

"Okay, Mama, that's not a problem."

Jenny was so pleased with her daughter's development. She was happy with her decision to move to London. The change of pace did wonders for all of them. After 3 years of being away from the island, Jenny longed to visit her home again. Although the opportunity arose several times, she opted not to go at the last minute, afraid of tampering with old memories.

Thoughts of her husband were still clear in her mind. Sometimes she felt angry with him for dying—sometimes she just missed him terribly. Jenny was still in regular contact with Ike, sending him books and finances for the youth center. According to

Ike, the Chloé Ford Center was still thriving in the community, and the children took full advantage of its resources.

The underprivileged children of the world were Jenny's passion. She began a campaign to collect and distribute books for children of all ages. Although many books came in, large numbers were rejected for their questionable content. Jenny also hired a team of people to screen the books. It was pointless, in her estimation, pouring nonsense into a child when there was so much good to be had. Jenny remembered the books that her grade school teacher loaned her. Had it not been for Ms. Trotman, Jenny would not have dared to dream big.

Cassie and Thomas traveled with their mother at least once a year, presenting books and opening study centers for the less fortunate communities. Jenny was proud to see how her daughter had grasped the vision. Cassie had genuine compassion for the children. Quite often Cassie was moved to tears as Jenny shared her testimony with the youngsters.

"Dare to read, dare to dream, and dare to reach for the stars!" she challenged them. What really moved Cassie was the countless letters of thanks and success stories that flooded the Foundation's mail.

The Ford Foundation had become a key resource center with distribution warehouses in three nations. "Every child should be allowed to dream and to pursue their dreams," Jenny frequently told her sponsors. She did and was thankful for the opportunity.

Between her children, her career, and the foundation, Jenny was a busy lady. There was a part of her that longed for companionship, though she dared not to spend much time entertaining those thoughts.

~Chapter Fifty-five~

O ne of the great things about Anton was he was always willing to include Thomas in his plans with Jenny. He knew that the two of them were virtually inseparable during her free time. Occasionally Jenny arranged for a sitter to come in for special occasions, whether it was work-related or a visit to the theater with Anton. Whenever Anton visited Jenny on set, the atmosphere became charged. Everybody noticed it except for Jenny.

"The man is in love with you, Jenny. You can't grieve for the rest of your life," Eric advised her. "Any other man would not be so patient."

Jenny shrugged off Eric's comments as she had done all the others. Anton was a great friend, nothing more—they simply enjoyed each other's company. Jenny insisted that their dates were friendly and not at all romantic. Anton was a kind friend, a consummate gentleman.

Quite often, Mr. & Mrs. Rodriguez would drop a few casual hints regarding Anton's feelings for her. Jenny dismissed their remarks as wishful thinking on their part. She was sure they were still trying to set their son up. Nonetheless, they insisted she was a part of their family. Cassie also thought that Anton was the best thing that had happened to her mom since her dad had died and wondered why they didn't make their relationship official. Jenny was finally starting to give herself some attention after all the years of strictly focusing on her children.

Mr. and Mrs. Rodriguez had become so much like family that Cassie often called them from school to keep in touch with the couple. Not long after, Cassie joined her little brother in calling them Grampa and Nana.

"It is less formal, Mama," she explained to her mother. "Grampa says it could also be destiny."

That was a touchy subject for Jenny. She was willing to admit to herself that she was very attracted to Anton but not to anyone else, for the moment at least. It was Cassie's last year in high school, and she didn't need to complicate it with a man in their lives. That's what she told herself every time Anton called, even though she looked forward to their lengthy telephone conversations.

Almost three weeks had passed, and she had not seen Anton. There was not as much as a telephone call. Even if he traveled, he called to chat for a while. Jenny missed him terribly and noticed that Thomas had grown quite attached to him and often inquired about his whereabouts. Jenny curled up on her sofa with a novel and a cup of hot chocolate.

"Oh Anton, where are you?" she sighed.

Jenny spent most of the evening daydreaming of Anton. If he were to walk through the door right now, she thought, she would wrap her arms around him and kiss him. Then again, knowing herself, she wouldn't. This was probably just a case of what was called absence making the heart grow fonder.

"It must be the music," she said, as the jazz sounds played in the background.

No, she thought, arguing with herself—it was his closeness she missed. His smell, the way he walked and talked. What he stood for. His character, as well as his somewhat old-fashioned beliefs... She even loved the way he interacted with the children. Anton's face flashed before her again and again. She was so busy playing it safe that she had literally pushed him away. The truth hit her long and hard as she sat holding her warm cup. She was in love with Anton and hadn't even realized it.

The doorbell rang. Jenny peered through the peephole. She knew it was Anton, his fragrance seeped through the sides of the door.

"Hullo Jenny, may I come in? I know it's late, but I had to see you."

Jenny opened the door wider for her friend to come in. Her heart fluttered nervously. She was grateful he was not a mind reader.

"Are you alright, Anton? You look like you've lost your best friend."

Anton smiled halfheartedly.

"I'm praying it won't come to that. I need some advice, Jenny, and you're the only person who can help me."

Anton followed Jenny to her living area. He tossed his coat onto the back of the chair. It was quiet except for the soft music playing. Anton picked up a book from the sofa and placed it on the side.

"This is a surprise, Anton. I haven't heard from you in weeks. Were you traveling?" she asked, curling up at the other side of the sofa.

"No, Jenny. I've been trying to sort out my thoughts... my life, really. Anyway, I need your help."

"I'm humbled that you would think I could offer any assistance. You've always been an encouragement to me."

Anton leaned over and took Jenny's hand.

"You underestimate yourself, lady." Jenny squeezed her friend's hand and moved closer to him.

"What is it, Anton? You know I'd do anything I can to help you." Anton gently caressed her hand as he spoke.

"I have a lady friend. I've been seeing her for some time now."

Jenny was thankful she was already seated. It would have been quite embarrassing to fall down in shock in front of the man with whom she had just determined minutes ago to be in love with.

"Jenny, even when we're apart, my mind is consumed with thoughts of her," he confided.

Jenny was stunned. She felt like the wind was knocked out of her, the palms of her hands began to sweat whilst her heart raced. She now understood why she hadn't heard from nor seen Anton in a while. He didn't belong to her, nor did he owe her an explanation for his private life. She had made it quite clear from the beginning that she was not interested in having a relationship with anyone.

Jenny tried to remain calm. She gently pulled her hand away from his.

"Have you told her how you feel, Anton?" Jenny asked.

"I've been a little too reserved in that area, I'm afraid. She's totally oblivious to me. I don't want to crowd her or frighten her away. What do you suggest I do, Jenny?" Jenny was at a loss for words. Her heart beat frantically as she tried to maintain her calm.

"If you feel that strongly about her, perhaps you should just find her and tell her. She's quite fortunate to have someone like you. She'd be a fool to turn you away."

Anton looked at Jenny soberly, "Do you really mean that, Jenny?" Jenny stood to her feet and began to walk away before he noticed that she was becoming emotional.

"I'm sorry, Anton, it's late, and I have an early morning. I wish you all the best with your lady friend."

"Jenny, I just poured out my heart to you, and that's all you have to say?" Jenny looked away from Anton, not wanting him to see the tears surfacing in her eyes. "Jenny, I drove around the block three times before I got the courage to walk up those stairs. I couldn't bear it if you turned me away. I've kept my distance for almost a year, Jenny. I can't any longer. I love you, and I want you to be my wife."

Jenny couldn't believe her ears. Was she actually hearing Anton say he loved her, or was she dreaming?

"Anton, what are you talking about? You just went to great lengths telling me you were in love with someone, and now...."

Jenny held her hand over her mouth. Anton was talking about her all along.

He took her hands, turning her to face him, "Now what do you say, Jenny? I followed your advice." Jenny felt overwhelmed—she couldn't hold back the tears any longer.

"Oh Anton, you big oaf... Why did you put me through all of that? You broke my heart. I thought you were seeing someone and had fallen in love."

Anton placed his finger on her lips to quiet her and pulled her closer to him. Jenny felt his love envelop her. She had finally let her guard down.

"I thought you knew I was talking about you, my love."

Jenny shrugged her shoulders, trying to hold at bay some of the emotions she was feeling. "I've not heard from you in several weeks, Anton. I thought you were avoiding me."

"I was," he said softly, enjoying the closeness he had longed for, for such a long time. "I was convinced that you didn't want to have a relationship, so I tried to get you out of my system—cold turkey."

Jenny smiled to herself, funny he should use that word. Cassie had called her a chicken a little earlier. It was another one of her conversations about Anton being the perfect man for her.

"Let me hear it from your lips, Jenny. Let me hear you say the words I've longed to hear for more than nine months."

Anton stepped back from Jenny and tilted her chin up. She felt as though she would melt staring into his deep brown eyes. Jenny didn't want to talk anymore. All she wanted was to feel his lips pressed close to hers. Her body ached for his.

"I love you, Anton," she whispered as his lips met hers.

Anton held her tightly, the warmth of his cheek and the musk of his cologne drenching her senses at every turn. "We were meant to be together, Jenny," he whispered. I don't want to spend another day away from you. Please tell me you'll be my wife."

"Yes, Anton, yes, with all my heart, I'll be your wife."

Jenny never thought she could possibly experience such joy again. Anton not only loved her, but he loved her children too. The quiet pain she nursed over the years was now gone. Her children would be thrilled to have Anton as their father. Jenny closed her eyes as she held on to Anton. She thought she had seen Thomas' face smiling at her.

Her heart warmed with delight as Thomas' last words resonated in her mind, "You must continue to live, Jenny."

Jenny smiled as Thomas' face faded lovingly away. She knew that loving Anton could never take away what she and Thomas shared. She would do as Thomas said and was now determined to live.

That evening after Anton had left, Jenny curled up on her sofa once more. Thoughts of her life on the island flashed before her eyes. She thought of old Aunt Bessie and her daddy. She even thought of her mangy old dog Rover. Jenny remembered the tussles she had in the mud by the village water pump.

Bloneva was right. The challenges she faced in life had strengthened and developed her. Life had handed her some mighty bad breaks. But, just as Bloneva had told her in the past, "If life hands you sour lemons, don't just stand there cryin'! Go find yourself some sugar and water and make yourself a sweet drink."

The problem was Jenny didn't know quite how to go about doing it, even though the advice sounded nifty. She didn't find out right away, but the more she prayed to God for help, the better the pieces of her life came together.

Tonight Jenny recognized her life had all the fixins' for sweet lemonade.

Tomorrow she would tell her children.

Other Books by Teri Bethel

My Marriage Matters

(Simple Keys to Enriching Or Restoring Your Marriage)

Before We Say, I Do…

(A Marriage Preparation Guide)

Saving Elianna

(A Supernatural Novella)

Native Talk

(A Collection of Bahamian Poems)

When My Spirit Sings-

(Inspirational Poetry)

Trapped On Kooky Island

(Children's Bahama Island Adventures) Book 1

The Case of The Missing Boat People

(Children's Bahama Island Adventures) Book 2

What's In Your Handbag, Girl?

(Materials & resources for making structured handbags)

19042476R00128